Riding the Wave

Riding the Wave

A Novel

by Frank Brian

Riding the Wave

Published by Pacifican Books
To purchase additional copies of this book, or other books by Frank Brian, please visit the following sites:
For eBooks: Amazon.com
For paperbacks: CreateSpace.com/5103717

Third Edition

ISBN: 978-0-9796379-5-7

Printed in the United States of America

Acknowledgment

To Ron and Maurice —
Thanks for believing in me, even before I did.

Thanks also to Patty, Robin, Bibbe
and all the rest of my friends
who encouraged me along the way.

Finally, my sincere appreciation to Stephen and Ryan for all the help in getting the original manuscript ready to print.

Wednesday

Chapter One

You can call me "Scott" or you can call me "Cuz," but don't call me "Scuz" or "Scuzman" unless we become friends. I'm beyond putting up with that at this point in my life.

I was born Scott Kuzman to parents who apparently didn't appreciate the potential social repercussions of naming me so, and I am of an indeterminate age (for the sake of this account)—just old enough to finally appreciate certain simple aspects of life, yet young enough to not have had the learning process dampen my enthusiasm for them.

I like (not in any particular order) surfing, sailing, sex, working with my hands, esthetics in specific terms and in general, philosophic answers, and I like hanging out with people who share these interests. I mention "sex" in this forthright manner not to push any buttons for or against it, but just to get it out of the way in terms of a self-description. I guess you could say I'm sort of an earthy, simple-pleasures type of guy, but I'm not into Internet porn or sleeping around.

Malibu, California is a beautiful place and I imagine it means something in particular to anyone who has ever thought about it. You've got your own image of it, I'm sure. But to me it represents some of the best, if not the best surf in the greater L.A. area. Of course the surf gets really crowded, in fact so much so, that it almost undoes itself.

That's why, when I got the call to trailer-sit my old buddy's doublewide in Paradise Cove for a few months, I jumped at it.

Paradise Cove is a southern California rarity that actually lives up to or surpasses its name. Nestled just below the northern hook of land that is Point Dume, it's the closest thing to a private surf preserve within driving distance of civilization that I've ever experienced firsthand. From its no-fooling-around steel access gates with their special residents-only keys to the north, to its sweeping primeval-like view of the Santa Monica bay and Palos Verdes peninsula fifty miles to the south, it always reminds me of the movie *Jurassic Park*, but without all the pterodactyls and T-Rexes flying and rumbling around.

My friend Ron Kimmel works for the studios as a set builder and when he gets a call to go out on location as he did just recently, with *Polly Want a Pirate Too* being shot in the Caribbean, he generally calls me to watch his place while he's gone.

His trailer at 275 Paradise Cove is one of the oldest in the park. Ron lucked into it during the relatively dormant real estate market of the early eighties and has never looked back. Being a truly fine craftsman, he has created little by little quite a gem of a property—a wraparound porch overlooking the ocean being his latest project. A hot tub on the roof (I still don't know how he got the building permit to do that) and a hermetically sealed garage to protect his Porsche against the coastal elements are two notable previous upgrades.

As a piece of "industry" trivia (entertainment, of course), there's a cozy restaurant down on the beach from Ron's place where *The Rockford Files* TV show used to set up a trailer in the parking lot—the supposed home of Jim Rockford. It always amused me to watch the show and see James Garner, playing the barely-getting-by private eye, living on the sand in Malibu.

But that's show biz for you, playing up the California myth. Gotta love it.

I don't know what, if anything, it says about my personality, but I've always been drawn to people who are, for lack of a better description, a "bit out of the norm"—artists, musicians, inventors, builders, outdoors types—you know, people who like to have fun in a constructive and esthetic way.

Anyway, Ron's that kind of person, and more . . . in fact a little more than even I like to admit to myself sometimes.

We met while surfing one day at Topanga Canyon more than twenty years ago—back before the surf shacks had been condemned and their Kahuna/Moon Doggie occupants evicted; back before all the vegetation had been cleared away and you could even tell there was a super hot surf spot there when driving by on Pacific Coast Highway; back before the parking lots (upper and lower) and the current spiffy lifeguard station had been built; and, most sorely missed of all, back before the current group of cliquey, butt-hole surfer bullies had moved in and started holding the place for ransom.

With regard to this last lament, it's amazing how just a few guys can work at ruining a good time for everybody else. But doesn't that seem to be the way that life can go in general?

Anyway . . .

It wasn't even a talking thing when Ron and I met that late summer day. It was just the easy companionship we both slipped into between waves, the common appreciation and pleasure of sitting out in the water with the rise and fall of the swell, the hum of the unseen traffic on PCH and the warmth of the sun on our bodies.

The water was liquid glass, the sky was Wedgwood blue with just a cloud or two for interest, and the surf was running five to six feet. Oh and the real clincher, only about eight guys were in the water. We surfed that day until we couldn't paddle anymore. We didn't know it at the time but things were about to start going downhill for the place shortly thereafter.

And so it's been with Ron and me since then—a timeless sort of relationship that you experience with few people in your life, like there is no beginning and there'll be no end. It's a soul connection, friendship, a belonging—simple, comforting and without analysis or explanation.

But just because Ron and I have some kind of timeless bond between us that neither one of us can really fathom, that doesn't mean he's well received or understood by many other people in his life. He's not.

Although he's a talented artist and artisan who is true to his own, albeit somewhat warped, code of honor, is MacGyverish in his ingenuity at dealing with the curves that life can throw at him, and drop-to-your-kneecaps funny when he wants to be, he can be a bit of a liability to hang around with too long.

In a compound word, he's a *risktaker*, and just because he seems to have nine lives, it doesn't mean the guy next to him does.

So even though I respect and admire him for his intelligence and abilities, and in spite of the fact that he's one of my oldest friends, I keep him at arm's length most of the time. For, you see, even I consider him a bit of a pirate, a guy who, in his own words, has a difficult time "coloring between the lines"—this self-assessment underscored by the fact that he went to prison once.

It was during a period of our lives when we had drifted apart due to him still taking drugs and me not. He wound up doing two years for something that he knew better than to do, but did anyway for "reasons" that had probably seemed sufficient to him at the time.

But even after "paying his debt to society," or maybe because of it, he's still wild-spirited in terms of his inclination to select out parts of his environment to fight with—unnecessarily so, in my opinion.

Unfortunately, until he sees this for himself, he's still got trouble waiting for him somewhere up the line. And because he's a big spirit, it's going to be big trouble.

In short, I've done what I can to warn him about this, and beyond that I don't go out of my way to spend a lot of time around him. I love him but I just don't want to be there when his shit hits the fan.

However, having said that, I've always figured that staying at his place when he was out of town was a safe bet. But then again, who knows.

Ron's Porsche goes very fast with very little apparent effort on its part. I love cars, but I'm not a "car guy" *per se*, so I don't know what year model it is or how big the engine is but I do know it's black, a "poon magnet" (according to Ron) and that we were clocking between 25 and 110 miles per hour all the way down Sepulveda Boulevard to LAX. And he still had a couple of unused gears left.

Ron is a taciturn guy (Latin *tacere,* to be silent).

"Not enough time for you to take me in your truck," was all he offered before we shot out of Paradise Cove in his Porsche, turned right onto PCH and headed south down to the airport.

OK, I can see that one of my little idiosyncrasies has surfaced. Ever since my mom taught me that words were the building blocks of communication, I've been on a campaign to improve my vocabulary. I started looking up words in the dictionary that I didn't understand—fancy words and simple ones alike—looking up every definition, using each definition in sentences until I got its concept and then finally checking out the word's derivation.

The derivation of a word is actually the cool part—seeing where modern words come from is very interesting. *Tacere* is also the root for the word "tacit," as in a "tacit agreement," an agreement without speaking.

If I hadn't gotten so much out of this over the years, I wouldn't bother mentioning it here, but since I have, I thought I'd pass it along.

The white zone at LAX is for loading and unloading and that's what Ron did. Once done (one bag), he threw me his Porsche keys, grunted "Thanks," and loped off to the ticket counter inside the terminal.

Standing in the street next to his blue-black roadster, keys in my hand, traffic streaming by me like L.A. coolness on parade, is when it hit me: His car is a poon magnet. With a tingle in my crotch, I eased the clutch out and merged into the flow home.

Thursday

Chapter Two

One particular physical universe phenomenon that is readily observable by most anyone is the way that things either *cohere* or they don't—things either stick together or, like the proverbial "dust in the wind," they disperse and go their separate ways.

I was absent-mindedly pondering this fact the next morning, as I padded over to open Ron's front door in response to a knock that had partially pulled me from my slumber.

Soft light particles streamed into Ron's trailer through the kitchenette window and illuminated tiny specks of dust held in suspension by a cohesion of air molecules which, as I cut a swath through the diminutive living room, at first parted and then rejoined in a playful swirl behind my bare upper torso.

My PJ bottoms cohered in a knot about my—

OH *NO*. I jolted, more fully awake

"Ron?" It was a woman's voice.

Tap, tap, tap. Again, soft tentative inquiries as if to say, "Are you there, are you up?"

If she only knew.

"Ron, it's Marney." Soft, youngish.

It's strange the way that you're able to articulate a complex thought in a circumstance where there is, quite literally, no time. But the thought that shot through my head at that exact instant concerned a theory that I had developed years previously, which, because of its nature, I had not yet been able to prove or disprove.

The theory involves the assumption that the degree of attractiveness of a female's disembodied voice (over a phone line, through a closed doorway, from another room) is directly proportional to the degree that she is *un*attractive in person.

I have often been beguiled by a female's disembodied voice. Once, for instance, a honey-toned customer service rep working for an Atlanta-based firm responded to my inquiry, "Why yes, Mistah Kuzzzzman, we hahve rahceived yowah piement."

After oral treatment like that, it was easy to see how phone sex had gotten its start. But in the soft afterglow of this extraordinary intercourse, the doubting-Thomas side of my manhood's inner self asserted, "Are you kidding? She's gotta be a whale. Hot chicks don't talk to you like that, even from across state lines."

It was true, hot chicks didn't talk to me like that. And thus the kernel of my theory was born. And of course, its corollary: Hot chicks treat me like shit on the phone.

Was this to be an opportunity for me to finally disprove this deeply disturbing assumption? To reassert the possibility that in fact, hot chicks might, or even do, talk to me pleasantly?

God. I thought. *Wake up. Focus.*

What had her voice sounded like?

"Oh, OK," she said, talking to herself from the other side of the door, her voice softly trailing off—and me envisioning her delicate mouth down-turned in somewhat sad resignation.

But then my mind shot back to my anatomical condition.

Damn. In my philosophical musing, I had totally forgotten my morning tangle—the still burgeoning knot of flesh, blood and flannel just below my waist.

"Jah . . . just a minute," I stalled, trying to balance the urge to stop Ron's mystery female caller in her flight, and yet at the same time wondering if I could will my lower anatomy into a presentable aspect in time to open the door.

The guy who invented Dutch doors had to have been a genius. Or was it a woman, his wife perhaps? Was he/she Dutch? Did it matter? NO.

In a flash, I sidled up to the lower half of the door and I deftly swept the upper portion of it open in an arc past my chest with a flourish and grace that surprised me. Like a bullfighter brandishing and swirling his scarlet cape at a befuddled bull, I completely deflected any possible attention Ron's female caller might have been able to direct toward my still inflated, yet finally beginning to flag, manhood.

But the next thing my mind struck was the fact that I now appeared, from the vantage point of someone standing ten feet outside the doorway as Ron's guest now did, completely naked.

Gawd. And the hits just keep on coming.

At this juncture, if I might, let me make a statement in clarification of the way I feel about the public display of the male and female body. I'm not a prude as hopefully my narrative has evidenced so far, but I'm not into the public promotion of sexuality either.

For myself personally, I don't like to lead with the "body suit" ("suit" as in playing cards). Not because I don't feel comfortable with the way I look, in or out of clothes, but because I don't feel the body alone is the sexiest thing about a man. It's the way you eventually consummate that attraction, for sure, but it's not the most interesting way to start it, is what I'm saying.

The same thing goes for the way I view a woman. It's a cliché to say that women are more attractive with their clothes on rather than off and I think that's true within the context of creating attraction. Obviously, however, once the initial attraction is established, things have got to progress from there.

So, having said this, I find the sexiest women are the ones who don't look like they're trying to be sexy . . .

OK, I just flashed back to my sister and her friends when they started getting into attracting boys—like the scenes in the original version of the movie *Gidget* involving the film's namesake going on "man hunts" with her pals. This thought changes the direction I was heading in slightly, but for the most part is well on the subject, so I'll just go with it.

As a young boy, based on the somewhat limited experience I had "clinically" observing women—primarily watching, as I said, my sister and her friends on numerous occasions while we were growing up—I nevertheless came to a certain firm belief. A belief so strong in fact, that I actually gave it a name: "The Theory of Chance Flirtatious Encounters."

This theory states that (drum roll, please) . . .

There is no such thing as a "chance" or "natural" sexually flirtatious encounter with a female if the female involved has any time at all to predict, prepare for and execute a strategy designed to maximize her sexual attraction potential to and on her unsuspecting, target male subject. PERIOD.

Example: There isn't, never has been and never will be an unfixed top blouse button on a woman's garment that allows by chance for a provocative hint of cleavage as said woman demurely leans forward to point out some "fine print" on a contract that a man is about to sign.

Never. Not going to happen.

No way. She planned it.

Another example: There are not a single pair of women's slacks in all of creation that have not been thoroughly scrutinized beforehand for their drape and cling characteristics should their completely "guileless" female occupant find it somehow "necessary" to bend over in front of some hapless sap she's had her eyes on at the office so as to "pick up some papers she's dropped," thereby "inadvertently" displaying the fine, fine, superfine contour of her now amply protruding rear end.

Again, it's not going to happen. Unh-uh. Deer-in-the-headlights time for that guy. Slam dunk. She out and out planned it. Guar-own-teed, mon cherie.

The shlub never even saw it coming.

And this brings me back to what I was saying in the first place: I find the sexiest women are the ones who don't look like they're trying to be sexy, not playing the body suit right off the bat, if . . . in light of my aforementioned theory, that is indeed possible. Oh well, one can always hope.

But of course, having said all of this, if I happen to meet a woman who's wearing nothing but a bikini and a smile, then all bets are off. So there you go, I rest my case.

And so, back to "reality."

"Oh," she smiled, evidently realizing I wasn't Ron.

Nice teeth . . . I thought. *Cute freckles . . . great body. OH MY GAWD, she's HOT.*

"Hi, I'm . . . er . . . not Ron, I mean you already . . ." I stammered and then, after pausing a second to regain a semblance of composure, "My name's Scott . . . Scott Kuzman. Ron asked me to house-sit for him while he was out of town." My face was getting red, nipples a bit nipply and my armpits starting to moisten up some.

"Oh yeah, he mentioned something to me about that," she said, smiling all over. "Well then, Scott ," she continued, closing the ten-foot gap between us with a grace that I can only describe as the female equivalent of the way Sean Connery moved in the early Bond movies, "I'm Marney. Welcome to Paradise Cove." And she shook my hand.

Chapter Three

Nacho Horta has worked with me for twenty years making the custom cabinets that I design for my clients. It was his page on my cell that had me wending my way back over Malibu Canyon to his shop in Van Nuys, San Fernando Valley.

Some people really have a thing about how "low rent" the Valley is, and after "living" in Malibu for the last fourteen hours, I was beginning to see their point. For starters, the temperature seemed to be running a good twenty degrees warmer as I approached the back side of Calabasas, just north of Mulholland heading for the Ventura Freeway.

The scrub grass that had been emerald green all through the winter and spring months had been dirt brown since July, and the stunted oaks scattered sparsely over the rolling hills offered minimal shade. It wasn't much to look at vegetation-wise, I guess, but this was the American southwest after all and, in its own way, beautiful.

Marney, I thought to myself as I drove.

Marney, Marney, Marney. I hadn't had my cage rattled like that for quite a while.

After I had been able to come out from behind the Dutch door and grab a T-shirt, I had recovered my social skills enough to invite her in for coffee. She had accepted, which was a pleasant surprise.

While I had set about getting things going in the tiny alcove that served as a kitchen, she had walked around the main room of Ron's trailer from wall to wall to wall slowly, deliberately and with apparent real interest, looking at the various pieces of art that Ron had collected there. Once satisfied, she had eased herself down onto the rattan and floral-print couch, tucked her tanned and taut legs up under her cut-off-jeans and looked pensively out toward the ocean.

Obviously she didn't feel the overwhelming need to chatter mindlessly in this situation, the way that I did. Because when she did speak, she made the most of it.

"You know . . . ," and then she turned her green eyes on me, "I think Ron's setting you up."

What? I thought.

She must have taken my stony expression, the way hard-boiled cops in noir movies affect, as a silent prompt for her to continue, for she did.

"Yeah." She returned her solemn gaze back to the ocean outside Ron's window. "I think he's actually off on a drug deal and he's got you pegged for his patsy, somehow."

My throat went so dry I could feel my tonsils swell and inflame, and I had my tonsils removed when I was eight.

When I finally wandered out to where Marney sat, coffeepot in my hand, struck dumb as an idol, she broke eye contact with the ocean once again and returned her somber gaze to me, assessing me soberly . . . and . . . and . . . she winked, the laugh lines around her eyes elongating and dancing.

"Man, I can't wait to play poker with you," she hooted with delight.

Have you ever felt embarrassingly socially deficient, completely outgunned wits-wise and at a total loss for any possible conversational gambit that might enable you to establish even the slightest pretense of interpersonal parity? Well, that's a bit wordy, but, nevertheless, I have and did, right then and there.

"Oh come on, Scott. Lighten up. I was just shaking your tree to see if anything would fall out. A girl can't be too careful nowadays about weirdos moving in next door to them. So, congratulations, you passed."

With that, she glided up off the couch, took my hands in hers and gave me a playful peck on the cheek.

"Here, let me make that coffee," she said. "You look like you've seen a ghost."

At that point in my reverie, my cell phone rang and it brought me back to the present.

"Nacho . . . yeah . . . no, I thought I'd swing by the shop first and then talk to Mortenson afterward. I'm just getting onto the 101 at Malibu Canyon . . . yeah, OK . . . yeah, see you in a bit."

What a pain in the ass this Mortenson guy was, I thought as I felt my gut start to churn.

Thirty minutes later I pulled into the lot behind Nacho's shop off Valjean in Van Nuys. It was hot, smoggy and, for California, humid.

What's the deal the last few years? I wondered, still on edge. Is it my imagination or is it more humid than it used to be?

Yeah, Scott, I thought. *It's not enough to be freaked out because the designer says the TV won't fit. Let's stress about "global warming" at the same time.*

Brilliant.

Nacho's shop was one of about twenty industrial spaces, backed up against the Van Nuys airport. A faint smell of aviation fuel wafted through the air as a Lear jet thundered down the nearby runway for takeoff, momentarily drowning out the wail of Nacho's machinery.

Compared to the noonday summer sun outside, the interior of the shop seemed dark, cavelike in fact, as my eyes struggled to adjust to the difference.

"Señor Scuz. *Como estás*?" bellowed Nacho over the whine of the shaper he was feeding wood into over in the far corner of the shop. "*Un momento*."

While waiting for Nacho to wrap up what he was doing, I looked around the cinder block room that for the last nearly twenty years had been my second home—my only home, in fact, for about six months after Shelly and I broke up.

Nacho and I had started out in a little place in Costa Mesa, just inland from Newport Beach, Orange County. But when Nacho's aunt died and left him a small bungalow in Canoga Park, combined with the fact that by then the bulk of our business had become centered in the greater L.A. area, we relocated the shop to its current location in the valley.

The strain of my having to cover all the ground between Orange County, where Michelle and I were still trying to make a go of it, and L.A. County where Nacho and our business had taken root, had proved to be the final nail in the coffin of my short-lived marriage.

Though I still obsessed sometimes about *what might have been,* the "marriage" between Nacho and me had proved to be both more enjoyable and enduring.

If only there were a way to make money from sawdust, I mused to myself, *I'd be rich now.*

When the howl of Nacho's shaper finally wound down, the low and labored hum of the swamp-cooler took its place, keeping the shop from falling into complete silence.

"Where's Rigo?" I asked.

"Oh, he took his wife to the doctor," Nacho replied, with a graceful "shit happens" shrug of his shoulders.

"Do you think it's for real or do you think he's out on a job interview?"

"No, it's for real." He smiled like the idea had crossed his mind too. "She came by here this morning and she's pregnant. He's a changed man, not fooling around anymore."

"Yeah, really? Well, I guess that's a good thing."

"Something had to happen to get his attention. I was almost ready to fire him."

With that, Nacho fell suddenly silent for a few seconds, maybe thinking about Rigo, maybe thinking about himself when he had been that age. But just as suddenly, he came back to the present.

"Say, let me show you what Mortenson called about," he said and left me to follow him to his little office space back toward the front of the shop.

"It's the flat-screen TV," he said over his shoulder, rifling through a bunch of papers on his desk. "He faxed me some specs today, but they aren't the same as what you show in your drawings. I mean, we're ready to start installing tomorrow but I wanted to check this out with you first."

When at last he found the paper he was looking for, he handed it to me and I studied it for a minute or so.

"Great," I said, but didn't mean it, the knot in my stomach tightening a couple more turns.

"It doesn't seem like it's the same TV," Nacho offered.

"It sure doesn't," I said, scrutinizing the fax a little closer. "Say, Nacho," I exclaimed, suddenly fortified by a thought I'd just had. "Let me run get my drawings from the car."

Thankfully, I'd remembered to transfer the briefcase containing the drawings from my truck to Ron's Porsche. If there was one thing I'd learned over the years about design work, it was that documentation is king.

With even a medium-sized set of kitchen cabinets, there are literally hundreds of measurements and details that have to be adhered to or the job will go south when you try to install it—something won't fit, or open or close, or, or, or . . .

Long story short, after Nacho and I conferred for half an hour, rechecking my original drawings (which the owner had signed) and then comparing my drawings against the TV specs that Mortenson had faxed Nacho this morning, it became clear that Mortenson had switched TVs in mid stream and was trying to pin the error on me.

Eureka.

Bolstered by that realization, I bid Nacho "*Adiós*" and departed Van Nuys for "Beaverly" Hills.

"Sorry, Morty." I smiled evilly to myself as I worked the Porsche through the gears up over Coldwater Canyon. "It's boomerang time."

Chapter Four

Fabian Mortenson, ASID, has an office in the Pacific Design Center on Melrose Avenue, West Hollywood. Driving the Porsche instead of my 1995 F150 pickup truck (which I love), I was amazed at the amount of admiring glances I got from the predominately male pedestrians milling up and down Santa Monica Boulevard. It appeared that not only was Ron's car a poon magnet but a "moon" magnet as well.

As a side note here, I'm not being patronizing when I say that the gay communities of L.A. and Pasadena have played a significant role in my success as a designer over the years. Although I'm as straight as the 5 Freeway on either side of *The Grapevine*, they've referred me around amongst themselves like a well-hung towel boy at a bathhouse, and I truly do appreciate that.

I have enjoyed being involved with their projects, I am thankful for their support and I am gratified that they have been happy with the work I have done for them.

'Nough said. But . . . gay, straight or confused, a bitch is a bitch and Fabian . . . well, was being a bitch.

As I approached Mortenson's little jewel of a boutique, I could see him through the window working a group of three 90210 matrons with—judging by Mort's obsequious demeanor—enough money, and the time in which to spend it, to give his entire shop an inventory transfusion. Out with the old baubles, in with some new—with a 200 percent profit right off the top, of course.

However, before I had even crossed the threshold of Mort's cozy little money trap, Dwayne, Mort's vigorous and severe assistant of recent months, was hissing in my ear in a somewhat venomous way. "Not now, Scuzman."

Were it not for the fact that Dwayne was attempting something fashion-wise with a pair of leg warmers that I hadn't seen done before, I would have been a bit intimidated. Dwayne works out quite a bit—in and out of the gym, I'm told.

"You see the *Lalique* piece that old bag is holding?" Dwayne eye-motioned in the direction of a large woman wearing what appeared to be a yellow muumuu with an inordinate amount of silver thread running through it. "That's fifteen K, and you know the rule." He looked menacingly at me. "When there's money on the floor, you *aren't*."

Judging by the rapidity and volume of blood flow that was coursing through Dwayne's carotid artery at this point, I could tell that a simple plea to wait until Mortenson was free was not going to get it done, so I reverted to "Plan B."

Raising my clipboard to my chest as if preparing to make an official notation, I said in a Broadway stage whisper loud enough to reach all the way down to San

Vicente Boulevard, "Well, then, I'm sorry. You leave me no choice but to notify the building's management." Fixing him with a theatrically stern expression, I added, "Nonpayment of showroom rent beyond a three-month period will simply not be tolerated." And I wheeled on my heels as if to leave.

The effect was electrifying.

The three Beverly Hills matrons literally shot past me as if they'd just remembered they were late for a Botox treatment, Dwayne's previously militant posturing was reduced to that of a little schoolboy who was about to cry in front of the whole class, and Mortenson looked like a fat grouper out of water, his mouth agape and big jowls working overtime, sucking nothing but air.

You could have heard a pin (or pen) drop; in fact I did, as the Mont Blanc Mort had been holding in preparation for consummating "the big sale" clattered to the marble floor at his feet, discharging a plume of blue ink across the toe of one of his salmon-colored suede loafers.

"You, you, *you.*" If apoplexy were a competitive sport, Mort surely could have been a contender. "Do you have any idea how much money you just cost me?" Furiously eyeballing me, he ranted on, "As Dwayne is my witness"—*What happened to God?* I wondered—"I'm going to sue you for everything you have, don't have, want to have or ever will have. And your skuzzy name is going to be *shit* in this industry. You won't design a doghouse once I get through with you. Dwayne, KICK HIS ASS."

At 5 feet 10 and 170 pounds, I'm not the biggest guy around, but I can hold my own in a pinch, and a closer look at Dwayne told me he was more a lover than a fighter, so I shifted my attention back to his "master."

"Mort, Mort, Mort, if it wasn't true, you could sue, but alas . . . ," I lamented, my face taking on a lugubrious cast, "your financial woes are legendary, second only to your harebrained, unethical and usually illegal efforts to solve them. I mean the Petrie job, after all." I wagged my finger at him admonishingly. "So let's cut the crap, it's a Mexican standoff."

And then it came over me . . . *Why the hell did I get into pissing contests like this—wallowing around in the dirt, trading insults with characters like Mort?*

I mean, what was the point? It never went anywhere, never resolved anything.

How about me exercising a little "bigness" in this situation, as my mom used to say to us kids? How about me being the one to let it go? Hmmm . . . now there was a thought.

And so I did, before I wound up saying or doing something that I really would regret.

"Look, Mort," I said, "I'm sorry about barging in here like I did. This thing with the flat-screen TV not fitting, and then me thinking that you were trying to make it look like it was my fault, well . . . it got me pretty steamed. So what I'm trying to say is . . . uh . . . I'm sorry . . . I'll, uh . . . call you tomorrow."

Without waiting for a reply, I turned and left both Mort and Dwayne standing freeze-frame, stunned silent, albeit with somewhat kinder and gentler expressions beginning to infuse their faces.

But no sooner had I exited Mort's shop looking for the nearest route to the street, than I ran physically (*SMACK*) into Bernard Weston of Weston Interiors fame.

Oh, great.

Weston was a well-known L.A. designer who, in recent years, had made a very nice living catering to the Beverly Park crowd. With homes in this tony, top of Mulholland Drive enclave running from 20,000 square feet for the modest folks to 40,000 square feet and up for the brasher, "I'm king of the world!" set, Mr. Weston had carved out a very nice little niche for himself indeed. One that I wouldn't have minded getting in on myself.

In short, Bernard Weston was one designer with whom I—under more genteel circumstances and with a more decorous meaning of the word applied—would have loved to have made "contact."

But, alas, a rosy first impression was not to be, for Weston responded to our current "introduction" by wailing in near hysteria to the muscular man who was accompanying him, "OH my God, Horatio, I'M BEING MUGGED."

At this, his companion, working somewhat to stifle a smile, leaned over to help Weston who had taken a theatrical header onto the carpet with the armload of fabric swatches he had been carrying.

"I'm terribly sorry," I offered lamely as I made a token move to assist Horatio in righting the little gnome.

"Well, you ought to be," Weston sputtered, sweeping imagined dust off the front of his tidy blue blazer, while Horatio retrieved his samples.

"No, no," I said. "I really am. I mean it's been a disaster today. I . . . well, I just didn't see you. I'm sorry."

Weston, at first merely appraising me with a piercing gaze, finally begrudgingly half-swallowed a barely audible "Well, OK," and motioned for Horatio to accompany him in leaving the scene.

"What's the West Side coming to?" I could hear him mutter rhetorically as the two men walked off down the corridor toward the escalator.

Shit, I muttered to myself. *What's the west side coming to, is right.*

After leaving the Pacific Design Center, I drove south on Robertson heading toward the 10 Freeway and started thinking about Mort.

The thing that had gotten to me about mixing it up with him was the futility of it all. It wasn't a question of whether or not he was "guilty" of what I had suspected him of. That didn't even bother me that much. What had really gotten me down was an idea that I'd been wrestling with lately: that behind Mortenson and all the shenanigans he was capable of, in fact behind every guy like Mortenson, was another guy angling for an advantage, who was just as bad, if not worse—and then behind him, another, and another, and another, and so on and on.

Mortenson wasn't really a bad guy at heart. He was just caught up in the game, a losing game, like I was. I mean, wasn't it time that we all started working together, helping each other out?

There was a story I was once told by someone that illustrates what I'm talking about here.

Once upon a time, there was a big inverted cone-shaped hole in the ground and its sides were covered with loose sand. On those slopes, crabs were struggling to climb up out of the hole. The only thing was, there were lots of crabs and they were crawling over each other, and on each other, and standing on each other's backs and heads, all in an effort to try and gain a foothold so that they could climb out. But it wasn't working, because none of them, not one crab, was getting out . . . or had gotten out.

Just as one crab would almost reach the top and achieve freedom, another one would climb up on its back to try and leapfrog past it. And when this happened, the first crab would tumble and slide all the way back down to the bottom of the hole where thousands of other crabs were in a teeming boil, going nowhere.

Some of the crabs had given up completely and were slowly getting churned down to the bottom of the pit where they were crushed and died—eventually "paving" the bottom and sides of the very hole they had at one time been trying to climb out of. And as time wore on, the hole was becoming blacker, slipperier and more of a merciless place to be for the remaining crabs who were still alive.

End of story.

Jim Morrison, that rivetingly charismatic poet/performer of the late 1960s was once quoted as saying, "No one gets out of here alive."

Well, a lie told in a beautiful way is much more appealing, beguiling and believable than one that is not, but it's still a lie. And as far as I was concerned, Morrison's assessment was full of shit—a half-truth, at best.

The full truth of the matter was probably closer to this: No one gets out of here alone, alive. At least that was my current theory about life, and why I was in such a funk.

Chapter Five

Earnest self-delusion—where one bullshits oneself to the point where they believe something outlandishly false about themselves—is one of the most entertaining aspects of human nature to watch, oftentimes hilarious and it's something we all do at one time or another.

I remember once going out to look at a job for someone who turned out to be one of the ex-wives of a nationally known sports commentator. She was legendary for having really taken him to the cleaners during their divorce proceedings (if one were to believe the ex-baseball player's constant on-air banter about her).

About halfway through the meeting, we came to the subject of the cabinet budget which, as I told her, I was concerned might run higher than she had originally hoped. At this point she took me aside, lowered her voice and with as straight an expression on her face as you could imagine anyone ever mustering, assured me, "Don't worry about it. I'm a giver, not a taker."

Well, I was certainly relieved that she cleared that up for me.

The reason I got off on this tangent is because after leaving the Design Center, I kept thinking about Mort and what I had said to him. But more than that, I kept thinking about my reasoning behind it—all that stuff about the crabs and Jim Morrison, and no one getting out of here alone, alive.

I mean, did I really expect to be able to take the virtuous high road with guys like Mort, or was I just kidding . . . ?

OK . . . Bullshitting myself about . . . *All right.* Bullshitting myself to the point where I believed something outlandishly false about myself?

Only time would tell. Because I sure couldn't.

When I finally surfaced from my thoughts, I was in the Marina. It seemed my emotional autopilot had taken over driving while I was thinking and I was thankful for that because I could immediately feel the place working its usual restorative magic on me.

Marina del Rey was originally conceived as a man-made harbor ringed with a huge apartment complex named after it, and if it wasn't . . . well it should have been, because that's what it is.

Over the last forty years, a lot of private residences have been built in the area as well, but even so, I would hazard to say that still more people rent there than own.

Another factor that has had a big effect on the Marina since the beginning, has been its close proximity to the, at times, low-end bohemia of Venice immediately to the northwest.

Venice was originally envisioned as an Italianesque entertainment destination for downtown "Angelenos" who on weekends could take the trolley car west out along Wilshire Boulevard (or maybe it was Santa Monica Boulevard) for a little relaxation and respite from the inner-city summer heat.

However, my earliest memories of the place, as a kid, were of a city on the seedier side—the period after Pacific Ocean Park had become a decrepit derelict of an amusement venue and finally been razed. And when the streets of Venice seemed pretty mean once the sun went down.

But yet a third factor played a part in ultimately shaping the character of the Marina. That was the fact that there was only so much oceanfront land in L.A. and *every*body wanted to have a piece of it . . . and all still do.

The net result of these three dynamics over the years had been a gradual gentrification of Venice—without it turning into a soulless "art colony"—in conjunction with a constant "downward" demographic pressure on the Marina, preventing it from becoming just another clubby, elitist enclave for the nouveau riche.

In short, I believe both Venice and Marina del Rey have benefited from their very unique relationship over the years. For they have both become places where one can "take a walk on the wild side" on one end of the social spectrum, live the "swell" life on the other, or, with a substantial percentage of both cities' populaces being just one forfeited security deposit away from throwing one hell of a lease-busting party, have a great time in the middle.

It's quite a place. Aside from the residents who live ashore in the marina, there are also those who live on their boats. Anywhere from two nights a week to year-round for those lucky enough to have permits to do so—and even some who don't.

One friend of mine falls into the last category in that although he does not have a permit to do so, he has lived aboard his twenty-five-foot cabin cruiser for the last five years.

Lifestyle-wise, he's always lived on the periphery of the mainstream. So, living the way he does, one whistle-blowing neighbor away from being forced to move, is for him nothing new.

However, to me, the humorous aspect of his situation is that although his total rent, with utilities, is somewhere around $500 a month, he's managed to secure through his status as a boat owner all the amenities of much-higher-priced accommodations—things even people who pay $20,000 a month for the mortgage on their beach house may not enjoy. To wit: full access to a private heated swimming pool with chaise lounges and a gas barbecue, full gym with showers and sauna, clean and spacious laundry facilities, ample free parking and a storage locker where he can store his bike and other stuff that won't fit on his boat.

True, his boat's a bit cramped. But otherwise, his lifestyle strikes me as being nothing short of a lordly bum living the high life in style.

The real kicker, however, is that because his monthly expenses are so low, he actually has the free time to enjoy living at the beach—a very rare luxury indeed no matter what tax bracket one calls "home".

My friend's name is Steve Smith and he's a house painter by trade, a fine artist by divine talent. Let me rephrase that. Actually, he's a fine house painter and a superfine artist, for he is beyond a doubt one of the best artisans I have ever had the privilege to work with.

That's his "up" side.

Smitty's downside, however, is that he's not real "clock-dependent," if you know what I mean. When he's working, he starts about 10:00 A.M., takes lunch about noon (for one-and-a-half to two hours) and leaves for home about 4:00. However, if he has to "go get materials," all bets are off as to when he's going to be anywhere.

Another thing that can blindside you when you're dealing with him is that sometimes he may not show up at all—because he's "observing a holiday" that no one except Smitty has ever even heard of.

I remember one time waiting four hours at a job site for him to show up, only for him to calmly inform me once I finally did manage to get hold of him by cell phone . . . that it was Leopold Day.

Leopold Day? I still don't know what that's about. Nor do I care. But hey, that's Smitty. As long as you keep that in mind, you're OK.

Anyway, since I had found myself down in the marina, I decided to make the most of it and try to get some work done. So I drove around to *Tahiti* where Smitty keeps his boat (all of the streets that service the various yacht basins in the marina have tropical names).

As a side note, I happen to own a boat myself, a sailboat, which I keep in Basin "F" off *Bali*. But I'll tell you more about that later.

I was hoping to catch up with Smitty because the media room cabinets that Nacho has been working on are going to be stained by him. Since installation of the cabinets was going to start the next day, I thought it might be a good idea to make sure Steve was still on-board, schedule-wise. A real good idea.

I was pulling Ron's Porsche into one of the parking spots right adjacent to where Smitty keeps his boat when I heard, "Hey, Cuz," from somebody coming up behind me.

I left the windows down a crack so the interior would continue to cool off, set the alarm and turned to see who was calling me: none other than the artist himself, riding up on what might have been the longest skateboard I had ever seen.

"Whoa, boy. Easy, Trigger," called Smith, talking to his skateboard as if it were a horse.

Just when I thought he was going to sideswipe a Bentley that was parked next to me, he did a graceful drop-knee cutback, back-pedaled to the rear of the five-foot-long board, stomped on the tailblock and dismounted—the wheels still spinning, but Smitty now standing behind the fully upright board with his forearm resting on its nose as if he were leaning over his backyard fence, talking to a neighbor.

"Howdy," Smith drawled, smiling at me with that goofy, country-boy thing he likes to affect sometimes. "I was just thinking about you."

Once I got over the shock of his dismount, I smiled back and said, "Well, serves me right, cause I was just thinking about you too. Did you have something specific or was it just one of those cosmic, *I was thinking about you, so you started thinking about me,* things?"

"Little of both, I 'spect." He grinned, working a piece of straw he'd been chewing on, over to one side of his mouth.

Where did he get a piece of straw in the Marina? I found myself idly wondering. Maybe it was a weed.

"Nice ride," he said, taking the piece of straw/weed/whatever from his mouth and motioning to the Porsche with it.

"Oh, that's Ron Kimmel's," I said, turning to admire the car again myself. "He's out of town and I'm watching his place. It's one of the perks of the job." Then, looking back at Smitty, I asked, "How about you? Where did you get that?" indicating his skateboard.

Now that it was up close, I could see that the board had an outrageously gorgeous surf image painted on the deck.

"That's incredible," I said, in real awe.

"Made it," Smith said nonchalantly. "Like it?" Really asking, not just fishing for a compliment.

"Yeah," is all I could manage, still caught up in the spell of the beauty of the board. "It's one in a . . ." Then, feeling the cliché was far too inadequate, I said, "It's a real beauty."

Smitty beamed from behind his "backyard fence."

"Thanks, man. I'm thinking of making a few more. You know, sort of like individual pieces of art—something I could put in a gallery. Maybe sell a few."

"You could surely do that," I said. "Do you know any gallery owners?"

"There are a couple guys over on Abbot Kinney." He motioned with his head in a somewhat bored fashion. "But I don't know, it takes a heavy bankroll to really make a go of a gallery. You know, a place where the owner doesn't cave in to selling shit because he's afraid of not being able to make the rent?" With that, Smitty gave me a *You know what I mean?* look.

I didn't entirely, but I didn't want to gum up the flow of the conversation, so I just said, "Big time," with as much conviction as I could work up on such short notice.

That seemed to satisfy, and he continued, "The only guys I know seem like they're all too broke to pull it off—in it for the *luuuuuv* of esthetics," rolling his eyes sarcastically. "For all I know, they'll be selling trinkets to the tourists within a month. Some of them already are." Then, hunching his shoulders in a gesture of futility, he concluded, "But, what are you gonna do?"

"Yeah, I know what you mean," I said. "Seems like you've got to die to make it as an artist."

"Spoken like a true believer."

"Afraid so."

"So what's the deal?" he asked. "You want to see the stain sample I've been working on?"

"Yeah, I was hoping you'd have something ready for me," I replied eagerly.

It was after 7:00 when I finally got onto PCH and started heading back up north to Paradise Cove.

Chapter
Six

When I pulled into Ron's I could see Marney through the window of her kitchen, so after securing the Porsche for the night in its moisture-resistant garage, I ambled over to visit.

"Knock, knock, it's Scott," I called through the open window, then added, in case she'd forgotten (not likely), "the guy house-sitting for Ron."

What an idiot.

Marney leaned into the window screen and called out, "Hi Scott, come in. Door's open."

Once inside, I saw that she had the kind of place where you could imagine the sun would be shining, comforting and warm, even when it wasn't any place else. Being a cabinet guy, I was immediately captivated by the wooden ship model on display at the far side of the living room. It was an English man-of-war about thirty-six inches long, detailed down to the tiny blocks in the rigging of the sails. There were about fifty cannons arranged on three levels along each side of the upper hull, all of them aiming out from under miniature top-hinged shutter doors. Up in the rigging, sailors clung to the yardarms tending to the sails, while others went about their various tasks on the decks below—all in full period dress.

"Where did you get this model? It's fantastic."

"That's *HMS Victory*, one of the most famous ships England ever put to sea. My grandfather had that made, oh . . . almost fifty years ago. He was a British naval history nut."

Wandering out from the little kitchen, she continued, "Do you know in today's dollars that ship would have cost about a hundred million dollars to make? The actual ship, I mean." Marney was now standing next to me, wiping her hands on a dishtowel. "Not the model." She smiled and wiped an errant hair from her eyes.

"I've had it since Grandfather died, and I never knew anything about it until the other night," she said, suddenly turning pensive. "It's kind of sad when you think about the amount of . . . of . . . living, really, that gets lost between generations—life experience that doesn't get passed along. Like what I could have learned from my grandfather when he was alive, but didn't take the time to. Anyway . . . ," she said with a sigh, at last returning to the present. "The History Channel had a show about it the other night. It made me feel a little closer to him . . . which was very nice." She smiled at the little ship now as if it were somehow alive.

"What did your grandfather do?"

"Uh, he was a . . . a rancher." Marney was inexplicably getting a bit evasive. "Had a small place north of Santa Barbara. You know, some cattle, stuff like that."

"Does your dad still work the ranch?" I asked, deciding to push it a bit further and see where it led.

"No, he actually works for a development company. They build custom homes."

"Oh really?" I said, my interest suddenly piqued. "Which one?"

"Eagleton Ranch."

No shit, I thought.

Eagleton Ranch was one of the last big family-owned development companies in southern California. I had read online recently that they were finally starting to do what the Irvine Ranch Company had done fifty years earlier down in Orange County about ninety miles south of L.A.: develop thousands of acres of pristine coastal ranch land into a literal "gold coast" of luxury housing tracts, golf courses, bicycle paths and upscale entertainment, retail and commercial venues.

The big difference with Eagleton's plans, however, was that the population north of Santa Barbara, where it was located, was still only about 10 percent of what south Orange County had been when Irvine started. Whatever their business model, it definitely wasn't going to be a high-density approach.

"That's impressive," I said. "What does he do?"

"Oh, he works on various projects as needed, but he's currently in charge of doing the preliminary site development for a fifty-parcel, mini-estate project. You know, five-acre lots, golf course, the whole deal."

My God, I thought to myself. *Five-acre lots.*

Eagleton's phase-one starter strategy was leapfrogging all the way to the head of the class.

Most residential developments in the L.A./Orange County area never even topped out at one-acre lots, let alone five. In fact, the term "estate" itself—synonymous with "McMansion" in the trades—had become almost meaningless in southern California through its overenthusiastic misuse by gushing real-estate salespeople.

Eagleton Ranch apparently figured they could change all that.

Wild.

"What about you, Nosey?" Marney's laugh lines crinkled as she smiled and headed back into the tiny kitchen area. "Tell me a little about yourself."

I brought her up to speed on my twenty-year career as a cabinetmaker—born out of the joy I had experienced in the woodshop classes I had taken at Newport Harbor High as a teenager, nurtured by my love of nature from growing up by the ocean, and then finally catalyzed by finding myself married by the time I was twenty.

At the time that Michelle and I got married, I hadn't had the stomach for any kind of work that required I wear a tie, so construction had been my logical and only alternative. And for me, it had been a great fit.

"If you don't mind me asking . . . ," Marney walked out to the living room again, "what happened with your marriage?"

Now it was my turn to squirm.

I had asked myself that same question hundreds of times and had never come up with a satisfactory answer. But there's a difference when someone else—someone who's interested and who cares—asks the question. It kind of puts you "in the moment."

At length, I surprised myself by responding, "I guess it was just lust and in the end, that wasn't enough." I felt the heat suddenly coming off me in waves.

Could it really have been that simple? I wondered, looking at the breakup in my mind, like some abstract painting that was finally coming into focus, finally making sense.

"Yeah," I admitted sheepishly, more to myself than to Marney. "I guess we just really liked having sex with each other. I mean . . . ," shooting Marney an embarrassed glance, I hastened to add, "we cared about each other too."

"Hey, it happens." Marney gave me an understanding smile and I felt some of the shame that I must have been feeling all along—maybe even since Shel and I had split—fall away.

But then something else from the past called me back.

"It's just that one day . . . ," I continued, "she woke up and realized I wasn't ever going to be the kind of guy who could give her the whole package—make the transition to 'Big Money Earner who could support a family in the South Coast Style.'" Hooking my fingers around the description with a weak snort of disdain, I continued, "So . . . what can I say?" I fell silent while I turned the memories over and over again in my mind. "She left," I finally concluded lamely. "Simple as that."

"Yeah, money . . . ," Marney smiled wryly, taking a step closer. "It sure can be . . ." But she let whatever she was going to say trail off, a tiredness of her own enveloping her face.

For a few moments we both stood there wordlessly, neither of us seeming to notice or be embarrassed by it. For we were both lost in our own thoughts.

As for Marney, I couldn't begin to guess what aspect of her life she was mulling over. But for me, I was thinking about the one saving grace to the whole thing with Shel—that she had decided to leave me before becoming pregnant.

The fact is, she'd done us both a huge favor on that account. There had never been any doubt in my mind about it. But in spite of that, the break had always left me kind of shaken—*Could I have? Should I have? Will I ever?*

When I finally looked up again, Marney, who had evidently surfaced from her reverie before I had, was studying my face intently.

"You know what you need?" she at last asked somberly. "Sushi." And with that, her entire face broke into a radiant grin. "I know just the place to get it, so climb up out of that funk of yours and meet me back here in ten minutes. My car, my treat."

It occurred to me as I walked back to Ron's trailer to change for dinner, I still didn't know anything about Marney, not even her full name.

How did she do that?

Chapter Seven

Sosumi! is a little sushi place on the ocean side of PCH, just south of the pier. However, this being Malibu where very limited space, exorbitantly expensive automobiles and sometimes whale-sized personalities all conspire to make valet parking *de rigueur* even for hole-in-the-wall eateries, Marney dutifully relinquished the keys of her little VW convertible to the valet and we started walking toward the entrance.

"What's the deal with the name? It sounds like *so, sue me!*" I asked Marney, half expecting her to explode with laughter at my formidable punsterish wit.

"It is," she replied.

"Really?" I said, feeling dumber now for having commented on the fact.

"Place used to be called *Yojimbo* in the early eighties—owned by Jimmy Ralston, a TV producer here in town. But he ran afoul of the health department over an incident with some blowfish."

"Blowfish?"

"A Japanese delicacy that can turn deadly if it's not prepared just right."

Yipes.

At this point, Marney opened and held back the door of the little restaurant for me (that was a pleasant switch).

"Jimmy fought it but wound up having to sell the place, his only stipulation being that when he did, the current name be retained." With that, Marney smiled and said, "*Bon appetit,*" and with a sweeping motion of her free arm, bid me enter the relative gloom of the little room.

Yipes on rice.

I must admit that though I profess to "love sushi," I adhere to a very limited selection in terms of the dishes I will order myself: cucumber rolls, tuna rolls (not spicy), California rolls and readily identifiable varieties of sashimi—no gooey, runny or sticky items, thank you. Oh, and tempura. Does that count?

In fact whenever I go to a sushi place, I am reminded of the limitations of my palate, feeling more like a "sushi pretender" than a full-fledged patron. It is for this reason that I always avoid the sushi bar itself, where I imagine diners "trade riffs," like dueling guitar players attempting to one-up each other, at ordering exotic and esoteric variations of the fare. It was therefore with some relief on my part that the hostess directed Marney and me to a corner table well out of the spotlight of the bar's center stage. However, as we passed the overly crowded bar, one of the sushi chefs hailed Marney by name and she responded in turn.

An ominous culinary portent? I hoped not.

Once we were seated, Marney said with some disappointment, "Darn. It would have been nice to sit at the bar. Don't you agree?"

Well, let's just put it this way, dinner turned out to be enlightening both gastronomically as well as personally.

As for the former, although Marney could hold her own with any sushi-slinger at the bar, she took it easy with me, building slowly from what I was already familiar with to more, dare I say, "interesting" items? In the end, I was slinging back exotics like the best of them—Bring on the blowfish!—washed down of course, with plenty of beer, sake, and water. I always get so thirsty when I eat Japanese food. It's the soy, I guess . . . and *wasabi.*

As for the personal side of things, I finally learned that her name was Margaret Easling, but that she had been called "Marney" after her great-aunt, since early childhood.

"How is it that a single girl . . . er, woman like you wound up in Paradise Cove?" It had been a while since I'd been on "a date," and I was pretty rusty.

This was a date, wasn't it?

"The trailer has been in the family since the sixties. As far-fetched as it may sound, Grandfather won it in a poker game. At the time, Point Dume itself was pretty uninhabited—considered 'way out there,' even by Malibu standards. The story goes that the owner held three kings, but that Chand pulled off a gut-shot straight to win it. The guy was pretty miffed because it had been his fishing lodge. He was a big surf-fishing enthusiast, but rumor had it that he'd also used the place to land a few ladies 'out of season,' so to speak. Evidently, he was married to some cold fish in town." Marney was laughing now at her own inadvertent witticism.

"Chand?"

"Oh, Chandler, my granddad—Chandler. . . uh, Easling." And with that, Marney looked down a bit self-consciously at her plate.

"Why is it that the couple of times I've asked you about your family, I get the feeling you've got something you don't want to talk about?"

Marney was silent for a full half-minute, working a trio of sashimi around her plate with her chopsticks like a game of three-card Monty. When she finally looked up into my eyes, it was with the beseechment of a very young girl who was afraid an intimate secret of hers had suddenly grown wings.

"Scott, I like you, and I . . . I just want to keep things as they are for right now. OK?"

That wasn't much to go on, but, *What the hell?* I thought. *Everybody has their secrets and they'll all come out in the end, or not. Play it as it lies, Scuzman. Ride the wave.*

"I like you too," I finally said and covered her free hand with mine.

With that, it was as though a little dam inside her broke, and I could see the tension release from behind her eyes.

"Thanks." She smiled.

When we at last emerged from the restaurant an hour later, I felt quite sated, to say nothing of relieved at having maintained my dignity while facing up to the wild and still wilder fish dishes that Marney had plied me with. I must admit she had an appetite for life that was quite free-spirited and alluring, and I could feel myself being pulled into her orbit—in fact, responding to her aliveness every bit as much as to her physical charm, which, as I alluded to earlier, was quite impressive in sort of a girl-next-door kind of way. It was like a part of me was awakening to, I know not what. Hope?

Or, maybe it was just the *sake*.

"Let's go for a ride," she said as we turned out onto PCH from the restaurant's parking lot and headed north. "I want you to meet someone."

Chapter Eight

I've often thought that riding in a convertible, next to a beautiful woman, on a warm summer night . . . Well, suffice it to say, after our sushi "date" I'd settled into a very romantic mood.

However, as I mentioned earlier, I was so out of practice with this sort of situation that I didn't dare assume that Marney's feelings were likewise, so I just forced myself to "relax" and enjoy the beautiful torture of the moment the best that I could.

Once Marney turned onto Zumirez from PCH and wound her way around to Grayfox, out onto Point Dume proper, the sparsely foliated palisades of the coast were replaced by a somewhat rolling mesa of land covered with a wide variety of medium-height trees and vegetation, giving the place the general look and feel of a peaceful orchard at night.

The "someone" Marney wanted me to meet turned out to be Colleen Mannes, a very well "maintained" woman for her age—not too flattering of a description, I'm afraid, but nevertheless fitting in her case (I'm guessing late forties). Tan and trim in bare feet, old jeans and a cotton pullover against the coolness of the seaside air, her shortish blonde hair was running grey, but attractively so. Marney and she could have been sisters? Cousins? (I wasn't going to pry).

Once Marney had introduced us, Colleen showed me around her place. Marney, who was obviously already very familiar with the various points of interest on our tour, padded along contentedly behind us.

There's a mantra in real estate that equates the value and appeal of a particular home with "location, location, location" and Colleen's place had all three in spades.

Situated on the south-facing palisade of Point Dume with nothing but the breath catching in my chest between me and the entire Santa Monica bay, it was indeed very nicely located.

It's hard to conceive of homes like this until you experience them. When you do, you tend to think along the lines of "the most," "the best," and so on, but in actual fact, there are countless homes in L.A.—to say nothing of the world—that cast a similar, wonderful spell, with or without an ocean view.

I guess what I'm saying is that, as with a beautiful woman, a beautiful home is not all physical. It's the spirit of the resident that makes the difference between enchanting and so-so. In this case, I had a suspicion that Colleen's own personal warmth and appreciation of beauty had had the biggest influence on her stunning home. And as I've mentioned earlier, I'm a big fan of esthetics. However, I'm an even bigger fan of people who create and apply esthetics to the world around them.

We had just rounded out our tour and sat down on the huge sectional in the living room when a somewhat scrawny kid (fifteen?) in black-and-white checkered slip-on sneakers, baggy blue shorts and a Raider's jersey idled up next to Colleen.

"Who's new?" he asked her but eyed me warily.

"Oh, hi Weeg. I didn't hear you come in," Colleen smiled and turned her gaze to him. "This is Scott," she said, nodding in my direction, "Marney's friend. Scott, this is my son, Weegee."

Strange name, I thought.

"Hi Weegee. How are you doing?"

"Stewin'," he replied, a bit glumly.

"Oh . . ." Not knowing which way to go with that, I responded in a somewhat bored manner, "Beats spewin'."

A tiny spark of interest registered in the boy's otherwise totally flat eyes, like a light had switched on in a room somewhere way in the back. "Or veggie chewin'," he ventured tentatively.

I thought about that for a second and had to agree. "Or trouble brewin'."

"Or bad tattooin'," he eagerly offered.

"Or cold snow shooin'," I asserted in return.

After a few more exchanges like that, it was apparent that I had somehow struck a chord with him, because his eyes lit up and a warm, goofy grin extended across his entire face.

"Man, you're p'awesome!" Weegee yelped gleefully, his sudden exuberance taking me totally by surprise.

It was like I had made a friend for life in twenty words or less, but I still didn't have the slightest idea what he was (we were) talking about.

Reading the blankness in my expression, Colleen clarified, "That's a good thing, Scott—*p'awesome—pretty* awesome."

"Oh . . . good," I responded noncommittally.

"*Positively,*" Weegee, all smiles, corrected his mother.

Without missing a beat, "Well, that's even better—*positively* awesome," Colleen glowed, apparently used to this.

"Well, there you go," I acknowledged everyone and no one in particular, looking first at Colleen, then at Weegee and then back at Colleen. The all-purpose smile I use for weathering stupefying situations like this now settled to roost on my face.

"Weeg has been with me all summer but returns to school in a few weeks," Colleen offered.

What manner of school, I wondered, *could possibly put up with this kind of verbal abuse?* But keeping the brightly colored soccer ball of conversation bounding along, I asked, "What have you been doing this summer, Weegee?"

"Surf's my turf. The waves are my faves. Girls come and go, but the water's my babe, I love her so."

"And Little Dume's a major plume," I responded wholeheartedly, referring to the name of the surf spot not 300 yards from where we were presently sitting—I could hear the waves breaking there now, in fact.

"Got to know it, gotta show it!" With that, Weegee became even more animated.

"OK, Weegee." His mom evidently understood what he was talking about.

"Scott," Colleen turned to me, "Weegee wants to show you his . . . well, I won't spoil his surprise." Directing her smiling eyes back to her son, "Just don't keep Scott too long."

"Fast track, right back!" Then Weegee wheeled and looked at me expectantly, bouncing like a jackrabbit on coiled springs.

The "surprise" turned out to be a new surfboard. Not that you would have noticed it among the dozen or so other boards of various sizes, shapes and colorations neatly stacked on a set of racks at the far side of the garage.

"It's a five-foot-one *Zippi Fish.* Mike made it for me personally and it rides like a rocket." Weegee evidently was so caught up in admiring the new board that his rhyming banter had taken a rest for a minute.

"That's really cool, Weegee. We've got to go surfing together some time."

"That'd swivel. I'll be out in the morning if you can make it." Then as if suddenly noticing his lapse, he covered, "Surf tomorrow, there'll be no sorry," his eyes searching mine for any sign of "I *thought* so" on my part.

But I let it pass, ending with, "Say no more, I gotta snore."

A look of relieved satisfaction crossed Weegee's face, and, with that, he worked me through a complicated handshake routine and we headed back to the living room.

Smiling lovingly at her son as we reentered the room, Colleen said, "Why don't you run along, Weegee? Marney, Scott and I have some things to discuss."

"Poncho knows, Poncho goes!" And with that, Weegee flew out of the room.

As soon as the boy was out of earshot, Colleen nearly levitated off the couch with elation.

"That's incredible, Scott. You had him jabbering a mile a minute," she said, regarding me now with what seemed to be genuine admiration. "I've never seen him take to anyone like that before."

I thought about that for a second, figured, *What the heck,* and replied, "Dare I say, that's p'awesome?" And we all laughed.

When you're on a roll, you're on a roll . . . and judging from the increased warmth with which both Marney and Colleen were now regarding me, I was on a *Kaiser*. Which was more than fine by me.

Once the small talk died down, we got to the reason Marney had brought me over to Colleen's in the first place.

"Marney tells me you're quite a talented cabinet designer," Colleen opened.

Catching my "how did you know?" expression, Marney offered, "After you left Ron's this morning and I was cleaning up the coffee stuff, I came across your portfolio. So . . . I took the liberty. I hope you don't mind. I brought it back to my place. You really have done some very nice projects, Scott. And the letters from your clients say a lot about your level of professionalism."

"Well . . . thanks," I replied, a little embarrassed. "It's not often I get help like this from people I've just met."

"Marney knew I'd been looking for someone to help me with my home office," Colleen said, looking appreciatively now between Marney and me. "In your case, I'm glad she took the initiative."

At this point, the three of us adjourned to an empty back bedroom in the ranch-style house where Colleen planned for the work to be done.

"I've been working on an old fold-up card table for so long that I'm about ready to go insane. I need a stable place to work," Colleen explained.

"What do you do?" I asked.

"I'm a writer."

"Not just any writer," Marney blurted. "She's Lydia Washburn." And she looked expectantly at me for the appreciative amazement she knew would be forthcoming.

However, when I failed to accommodate, she prompted, "*Corset Strings of Love*, *A Man Around the Manor* . . ." Still nothing from me. "*Reindeer of Love*?"

"I'm . . . ah, sorry, they don't ring any bells. I'm afraid I really haven't been keeping up on my reading," I tried to appease.

"Marney," Colleen lightly chided. "They're probably just not the kind of books Scott would be familiar with." Then, looking at me, "They're bodice rippers, you know, the kind of books with Fabio on the cover." Me still blank. "Romance novels."

"Ohhh." A feeling of relief settled over me at finally knowing what they were talking about. "You mean, like with a character named Heathcliff who lives in a castle overlooking the Scottish moors? He's been mourning the untimely death of his child bride for the last two years, so when Lilly, the heroine of the story—a graduate student from Philadelphia—comes into his life, things really start to steam up and get horny for everybody? But in a very dignified and demure kind of way, of course."

"Exactly!" exclaimed Marney and Colleen in unison, laughing hysterically.

"My ex-wife used to read those. I always suspected they were churned out by cigar-chewing sportswriters from the *L.A. Times*—hardboiled hacks just supplementing their income. It's comforting to see that in at least your case, I was wrong."

"Yeah, those guys have been cutting into my action for years." Colleen laughed heartily. "That's why on the new project I'm starting, I want to have a nice office."

"New project? I didn't know you were working on another book." Marney's interest was spiking. "What's it going to be called?"

"My editor came up with an idea for a story set in Ireland during the potato famine," replied Colleen, her green eyes glazing over a bit as she contemplated it. Then as if suddenly "returning to America," she smiled and said, "The working title is *A Bumper Crop of Love.*"

Now that sounds like a ripper to end all bodices, I thought.

I made an appointment to meet Colleen at her place along with another designer she was interviewing the next day at noon, and then Marney and I left.

Chapter Nine

"What kind of name is Weegee?" I asked as Marney and I motored back down PCH toward Paradise Cove.

"Oh. Wilhelm Jedadiah—Weegee. We're so used to it that I sometimes forget what it must sound like to others."

"That certainly is a mouthful. I can see why you nicknamed him."

"My great-grandfather's first and middle names," Marney stated matter-of-factly, keeping her eyes on the road.

So the resemblance between Marney and Colleen *was* familial.

Curiouser and curiouser.

"What did you think of Colleen?" Marney flicked me a glance.

"I like her. What a house. Did she decorate it?"

"For the most part, yes. But since she's changing the carpets and window treatments throughout, as well as doing the office, she thought she ought to call somebody else in to help her with it."

"Has she found anybody?" I asked, purely out of politeness—"designers" can be a real . . .

Oh, never mind.

"She's been in touch with a man named Bernard Weston."

Ulp.

"He seems a bit pompous to me, but it's not my call. Have you heard of him?"

"The name rings a distant bell,"

A diving bell, I thought—*going down, down, down . . .*

"Oh and another thing," Marney blurted out, suddenly genuinely excited. "He owns an art gallery in Santa Monica—on Broadway, just east of Lincoln. Isn't that great? I thought I could talk with him about some of my stuff." Then, looking questioningly at me, "You knew I was a painter, didn't you?"

"I didn't." But the lack of previously knowing didn't decrease my enthusiasm for hearing so—not *one iota.* On the contrary.

All the rest of the way home, Marney and I talked excitedly about her paintings and her plans to sell them. By the time we had pulled up the gravel driveway alongside her trailer, any concerns I'd had about working with Weston had been, for the time being at least, completely forgotten. Nice.

"Oh," Marney said as she turned off the ignition. "Why don't you come in for a second and I'll give you your portfolio? You're going to need it tomorrow."

While Marney wandered off to the back of the trailer to retrieve it, I ambled over to the model of *HMS Victory* to take another look at her. There, behind the lamp next to it, was my job book. *That's strange,* I thought, *I hadn't noticed it earlier this evening.*

"Hey, Marney," I called to the door that she had just exited through, but she was already gone, so I picked up the book and settled into waiting for her to return.

To pass the time, I started flipping through the pages—"my back pages," as Bob Dylan put it.

God, it brought back memories—good ones and some not so good—like the time when Shelly had finally left me in the middle of the Harris job. That had been a tough time. But now, looking at the photograph of the old-English pub I had designed for Nate Harris' eighty-year-old father, you would never know it.

Nate's dad had wanted to "spend some more time with his buddies from the war," the real good ones he had shared laughs with at the pub they had frequented in England between bombing runs over Germany—none of whom had survived the conflict.

I could remember the effect that the finished project had had on Nate's dad—profoundly sad in a perfect kind of way—the design solid, the craftsmanship clean, his remembrances complete.

Yeah, for twenty years the work had always been constant, had always been good—the one stable thing of value in my life. *But had it been enough?* I wondered.

Had it been enough? Sitting there with my life in my hands, I found myself hoping so.

But just then, Marney's voice brought me partway back to the present . . .

"I have a firm rule about not sleeping with a guy on the first date."

When I looked up from my portfolio to see her wearing nothing but a nipply nightshirt and a smile . . . I came ALL the way back.

"But I figure our date ended when we left *Sosumi!*. I'm not sleepy anyway."

BOING.

Afterwards as I lay next to her, listening to the soft murmur of the surf and the gentle sound of her breathing, I wondered what I had done "right" to win the attention and favors of such a winsome lass as Marney. After all, there must have been something.

I mean I was the same guy that I had always been—dork or "cool guy," depending on how I looked at myself. Or maybe there was a third alternative . . . something in the middle that I hadn't considered before . . .

I was still trying to figure that out when I fell into a deep, restful sleep.

Friday

Chapter Ten

A "point break" is a surf spot where one end of the beach extends out into the ocean, forming a crescent-shaped inner bay. The advantage of this type of shoreline configuration in surfing is that incoming waves break out at the tip of the point first and then wrap into and peel off all along the crescent inner beach, affording a longer and often superiorly shaped ride.

Little Dume is a point break that faces due south and consequently breaks best in the late spring to early fall months when swells originate primarily in the southern hemisphere.

Another geological feature that affects the surf at Little Dume is a series of several underwater, mesa-shaped rock formations about ten feet in diameter situated along the route that the waves follow as they rush shoreward.

Depending on the tide (deep water or shallow), these formations, though always submerged, are anywhere from a foot to five or six feet below the surface. The effect as a swell passes over them is to suddenly jack the face of the wave up to a much steeper pitch, adding an extra element of challenge to riding it.

As I walked the mile and a half up from Ron's trailer to Little Dume, my surfboard under my arm, I could see that it was breaking about four feet with occasional six-foot sets coming through. The sun had risen half an hour before and the entire Santa Monica bay had a crisp, golden glow to it.

While paddling out, I looked over and saw two guys in the water out at the point where the waves were humping up prior to breaking. I recognized one of them as my good friend Skip Howard from countless surf sessions together.

Just then he wheeled his board shoreward, took three quick strokes and dropped into a sleek, thick six-footer. As the face of the swell steepened, he pushed up to his feet and shot all the way down to the bottom, going faster and faster, heading straight in toward shore. Finally, like slalom water-skiers do, with his whole body leaning out over the water, he cranked a big graceful turn to his right, angling away from the cascading peak behind him, and started heading down the shoulder of the wave that was extending out in front of him now, parallel to the shore.

At this point, the wave that Skip was riding passed over one of those submerged rock formations and the face of it jumped up and hollowed out for about fifteen feet ahead of him—a shimmering wall of greens and blues—and he really started to fly.

The faster he went the higher his board rose up the face of the wave, higher and higher, until at last just before the wave threatened to pitch him out "over the falls," he casually walked forward on the deck of his board until both feet—all ten of his toes—were curled neatly over the nose.

With this final maneuver, his ascent up the face slowed and then at last stabilized in a perfect equilibrium of forces—the pocket of the wave—and he held that stance, angling toward me with his back slightly arched, the wave peeling off just behind him all the way across the inner bay.

Classic.

I had just paddled out over the shoulder of the wave he was riding when he yelled in exhilaration, "Yoooooooo Scuuuuzman!" and shot past behind me.

"Yoooooooo Skiiip!" I yelled in response, turning and continuing to watch him from the back side now of the shorebound wave.

It's great to be in the water with Skip because his love of the sport is so infectious. He's a good friend too.

Skip and I started surfing together ten years ago, just about the time that southern California coincidentally went into a deep recession and my cabinet business was really hurting. At the time, I was still using a board that I had "outgrown" (gained too much weight for) but yet couldn't afford to replace (I was that broke).

Anyway, one day Skip asked me if I wanted to go down with him to Becker Surfboards in Malibu, "to check out a new board." Skip always liked to maintain a "quiver" of five or six boards for his own use, so I didn't give it any thought.

Long story short, we walked out of there with a beautiful new surfboard, which Skip then proceeded to tell me I could "borrow"—indefinitely.

Well, I've used and loved that board ever since and I eventually paid him back for it—over his protests, of course—but I've often thought about that, and I've got to say it's one of nicest things anyone has ever done for me. So yeah, he's a good guy.

Anyway, just as I turned back around to resume paddling out to where the waves were breaking, I saw the second surfer. He was wiry and slight, a young boy for sure, and I didn't know who he was until I recognized the board—the one I'd seen just the night before.

Weegee had caught another six-footer from the same set that Skip had, but his take-off was a bit different, to say the least.

Instead of a long board like Skip's nine-footer, Weegee's was just an inch over five feet and he caught the wave by quite literally dropping in like a guy standing up in a kayak going over a waterfall—free-falling from the pitched-forward crest of the wave all the way down to the bottom of its trough—with a few tons of liquid kinetic energy in hot pursuit. Only, Weegee got to the bottom of the wave first . . . and that's all the head start he needed.

The instant he landed, he transferred the entire ninety-five pounds of his body's bulk to his inside rail, snapping the board into a right-hand turn so fast that the avalanching water he had been a part of just a nanosecond before crashed harmlessly just inches behind him.

And the race was on.

A quick series of three or four jackknife turns—back and forth, back and forth along the bottom of the wave—earned him some much-needed speed, and with that, he started to climb back up the face of the barreling swell.

Finally, one more thrusting turn got him into the "sweet spot" of the tube . . . for a second . . . but by then his board was going so fast he actually started to outrun the wave, screaming toward the flat water of the wave's shoulder.

Recognizing this at the last instant, his board just inches from the top of the swell, he lay down fully on his back to slow himself, dragging water and foam behind him in his wake, and somehow—with his feet still out in front of him all on their own—he managed to execute a full roundhouse cutback, steering his board 150 degrees in the opposite direction from where he had been heading just milliseconds before.

I couldn't believe my eyes.

Now racing back into the tube like a trusty horse rescuing its master in one of those old westerns, Weegee's board picked his body up when it passed him and he snapped back upright "into the saddle," screaming downward once again toward the thunderous whitewater.

He gained the bottom of the wave in less than a second, and when he did, he shot out in front of its exploding rainbow, skipping across the surface of the trough like a runaway water-skier. When his board had reached the highest speed that the wave could produce, he hunkered down into a huge bottom turn that sent a rooster tail of water, fifteen feet into the air.

His rise back up into the maw of the tube was immediate, and when he got there he dragged his right arm to slow himself down, to keep himself from outpacing it. And this time his efforts were rewarded with his own private key to "the green room"—front row center to the innermost barrel of the top-to-bottom tubing wave.

He rode that way for what seemed like forever, a snapshot of eternity frozen in time, until at last the wave's power started to dissipate and fall in on itself, and then in a final flourish Weegee shot up, out and over the top of the remaining gently sloping shoulder.

But he kept on going . . . skimming for a good twenty more feet out into flat water until, at last, the wave's inertia finally completely spent, he sank (*glunk!*), board and all.

"Weegee, you the MANG," I hooted as his mop of scraggly hair surfaced. "The Mang," I repeated almost to myself.

What a ride.

"Thanks." Weegee smiled as he paddled up to me. "I am the Mang."

And we both laughed.

Surfing is something that can really set me free—really break the hypnotic grip that life sometimes gets me in. When the surf is running six to eight feet, it's like what I would imagine it must have been to be a cowboy riding a horse in and amongst a herd of wild buffalo at full run—a lot of power moving all around me, untamed and alive.

And I'm only what I would call a recreational surfer—it's quits for me when it gets over eight feet. I can only imagine what it's like for guys who ride really big waves—only imagine, and shudder.

I guess what I'm trying to say is that once I get past the fatigue and the pain, the fear and the thinking, I arrive at what can only be described as the spiritual—a state powerfully unique and independent from the other side of my life, that for so much of my time engulfs and holds sway over my thoughts and dreams.

Now that's living.

And the only thing that gets me down about this from time to time is when I hear some idiot I run into on the street . . . or see some A-hole on TV holding forth with the "you are a brain" theory, attempting to "explain" and dismiss this experience as merely "chemical reactions due to the heightened activity of the body."

That's just so far off the mark. The truth is, we live in very materialistic times—and I'm not just talking about money, *bling* and Hummers.

No, we live in a time where in spite of the technological advances that Man has made, "psychiatry" (Greek *psyche* 'soul' + *–iatry* 'healing') still pronounces Man to be merely a piece of meat, and not a spiritual entity at all. And that's so wrong. In fact, if there ever were a time for Philosophy, Religion and Science to stop bickering amongst themselves—to finally step up to the plate together on behalf of the Spirit of Man and hit one out of the park—it would be NOW.

It would truly be now. But in the meantime . . .

Skip, Weegee and I had the waves to ourselves the rest of that glorious morning. And we made the very most of it that we could.

That was a good thing because although I didn't know it at the time, I was going to need some happy thoughts to fall back on over the next couple of days.

Chapter Eleven

I was just getting out of the shower after coming home from surfing when my cell phone rang.

"Hey, Scuz!"

It was Ron on the line, the guy whose trailer, Porsche and—come to think of it—neighbor I had been enjoying for the last couple days.

"To what do I owe the pleasure of your call?" I responded.

"Cut . . . crap . . . man and . . . isten . . . me . . . ," was all I could make out.

"You're not coming through too well," I said. "Why don't you step outside?"

". . . am outside!" Ron screamed from his end of the frayed connection. "There's a . . . hurrica . . . the Gulf. I'm . . . coming home."

And then the line went dead.

Ron had always been a man of few words but this was ridiculous.

I walked over to his TV and turned it on.

"... Ned ... does it seem to you now?" one newscaster in a cozy studio in Burbank was asking "Ned Somebody" in Jamaica.

"Well, Bawwwwb . . . ," the reporter's rich baritone began. "As you can see . . ." And the camera cut to Ned Whoever.

Oh, "Ned Boulder," the letters at the bottom of the screen now informed me. Ned was holding a microphone and a palm tree with his left hand, and motioning down the beach with his right.

"There's quite a bit of meteorological mischief being kicked up by Hurricane Annie."

In the foreground of the shot, the camera now trained somewhere down a deserted beach, I could make out an old VW beetle buried up to its hubcaps in sand.

"And to think that this ferocious storm came up out of nowhere," Burbank Bob prompted, in mock urgency.

"Yes, ferocious is right and nowhere is a Roger as well. In fact," Ned continued, "we've been trying to talk with some of the locals here to get their reaction. Oh, here we go. Mr. Hudson." Ned, winking into the camera, added, "I was speaking with him earlier. Er . . . Mr. Hudson."

At this, the camera swung on to a short, fat man in a pair of Bermuda shorts holding a beer in his hand, a look of amusement on his face.

"Mr. Hudson," Boulder cried. "What is your reaction to all the destruction that is occurring here?" he asked, shoving his microphone into the man's face.

"Well, Ned." The man's beer-slicked lips made contact with the black foam ball on the tip of the instrument. ". . . a really fantasic time . . . here. It's a . . . that . . . would . . . if I were . . . mangy seagulls . . . everywhere . . . and . . . New York City." And then he took another swig of his beer, a look of supreme satisfaction infusing his florid face.

"Thank you, Mr. Hudson," Ned crowed.

Turning back to face the camera, Ned pronounced, "Well, there you go, Bawwwwb. I couldn't have put it any clearer myself."

"Uh yes, Ned, I'm sure you're right," Burbank Bob interjected. "But say, is there any update on the cast and crew of *Polly Want a Pirate Too*? A lot of viewers have been calling in for information and the last word we had here was that they were having a pretty rough time of it."

"*Arrrh.* A rough time is right, Cap'n Bob," Ned quipped, mugging like a pirate in a rum commercial. "Our reports have been kind of sketchy but from what we understand, Hurricane Annie plowed right through their set sometime late last night. The cast and crew escaped unharmed but the pirate ship is a complete loss. Of course the producers and stars hopped their Gulfstreams home, but it'll be a long haul back to L.A. for everybody else—what with the FAA suspending all commercial flight into and out of the entire area.

"So on that unfortunate note," Ned saluted the camera cheerily, "it's margarita time here at the KWAM Destruction Alert Team's Situation Station. Adios and back to you, Bawwwwb."

At this, the camera feed switched back to the Burbank studio—a wide shot of Bob now being joined by a hot-looking Asian chick with big tits.

"Joining us now is Jenny Sakuda, our KWAM Destruction Alert Team meteorologist. My God, Jenny."

Fake concern was seeping from every pore of Bob's deeply tanned face. "What do you make of all this devastation?" The camera now moving in tight and low on Jenny's face and bountiful bustline.

"So, so sad. Wind blow so hard. Waves, they so wet."

"Uhh . . . Yes," Bob somewhat tentatively responded off camera, the TV screen still riveted to Miss Sakuda's chest.

"So, so sad." The camera moving in even tighter and lower now, finally cropping off her face altogether, save for her pouting lips.

And then Miss Sakuda's upper torso turned toward Bob, still off camera, her nipples noticeably erect in profile.

"So sad, so hard, so wet," she earnestly repeated in a sing-song voice.

At this point, what seemed to be a jostling match over control of the camera ensued; one second, Jenny's boobs filled the screen, the next moment a transfixed Bob staring at them.

Back and forth the camera whipped until, at last . . . a view of the studio ceiling filled the screen, then . . . cut to commercial.

"Jesus," I said and turned the TV off in disgust, grabbing my portfolio and heading for the door.

I had had an ominous feeling about today's meeting with Bernard Weston anyway, but after watching the news, I felt even more on edge.

In fact the thought of getting together with him at Colleen's, after our disastrous "first meeting" yesterday at the Design Center, now loomed in my mind like a "category 5" worry system.

Who was it that said, “In moments of one’s greatest failings, exist even greater opportunities to yet succeed?”

Anyone? No one? I made it up?

Whoever it was, I was about to put it to the test.

Chapter Twelve

As you may have already noticed, I can become somewhat testy at the mention of designers—to say nothing of having to get together with one, like today at Colleen's.

But since I'm on the subject, let me lay out my case from my perspective as an artisan and a designer myself and see if I can't present a sensible argument in my defense.

First of all, being a designer is a tremendously creative and highly demanding art form and profession, and I hold those who can perform the functions of it in the utmost respect and admiration.

The only problem is that in all the years that I've been designing and making cabinets, bad designers have outnumbered, by far, good designers. And one day years ago, being the more or less theory-oriented egghead that I'd always tended to be, I decided to set about trying to isolate what made many designers so damnably awful, in my opinion.

So I began to study designers from near and far, high and low, here and fantasyland . . .

And finally, at the cost of literally hundreds of wasted man-hours, tens of thousands of dollars in lost earnings, countless beyond countless swallowed expletives and a fantastic amount of teeth-gnashing, I isolated four principles, which, for the sake of brevity, I have listed in bullet format below.

- A good designer knows what he or she wants; a bad designer knows what he or she doesn't want.
- Esthetics is only one of four more or less equally vital elements to successful design—the other three being function, time and money.
- A designer must have the ability to draw or use samples, mock-ups and/or pictures to accurately and fully communicate what the heck he or she is talking about.
- And a fourth, which is pretty much just my opinion: People don't hire designers because they "need to be told what they like" (and potential clients who do should be avoided). They hire designers because they need help articulating what they like.

In short, my whole beef with designers was pretty much summed up in violations of those four points.

But having said all that . . .

By the time I parked my pickup truck for my twelve-o'clock appointment with Colleen and Bernard, the knot in my stomach had become Gordian, so I just cut it.

To hell with it. *Whatever happens, happens,* I thought to myself as I threaded past Weston's Range Rover and walked on into Colleen's open front door.

"I think that would be a truly *gutsy* detail," a man with his back to me was saying to Colleen. "In fact, if you carry that all along the ceiling . . ." I could now see that it was Horatio speaking, the man who had been with Bernard at the Design Center yesterday. "That would bring both elements together."

"That's a great idea," Colleen enthused, and then, noticing me as I rounded the couch into the living room, said, "Oh, hi, Scott."

Smiling warmly at me, she looked back at the pair of men in front of her. "Horatio, Bernard, this is Scott Kuzman, my cabinet designer," she motioned over their shoulders in my direction.

Bernard whirled around with a smile on his face that died immediately in its tracks.

Bam.

Horatio, on the other hand, seemed to take my reappearance in stride, a hard-to-read smile spreading across his otherwise tight lips.

"Mr. Weston, Horatio, I believe we've . . . ah, already met," I offered, willing and hoping to bury the memory of yesterday's debacle right then and there.

To further this end, I crossed the distance between us and extended my hand to Weston, nodding an acknowledgement at Horatio in the process.

I could tell Bernard wouldn't have taken my hand at all had I not preemptively offered it to him in front of Colleen, but then, hey . . .

C'est la vie designeur.

I don't make the rules of civil commercial discourse, I just try to live by them.

"Scott, is it?" Weston grimaced, as if it gave him a sharp pain somewhere inside to say it. "I don't believe

I caught that at our last, uh . . . meeting." He flicked his eyes toward Colleen to see if his covert dig had escaped her notice.

It had.

On the contrary, Horatio extended an open hand to me and said amiably, "And I don't think you got my name—Blaire, Horatio Blaire. I manage our gallery and go out on site with Bernard from time to time."

As we shook hands, I couldn't help feeling I was being worked with some variation of the "good designer, bad designer" routine . . . or would it turn out to be bad designer, worse designer?

Time would tell.

So I smiled at Blaire guardedly and then, turning to Colleen, embraced her warmly and sincerely.

"Hi Colleen."

"Scott. It has been such a long time." She giggled as she hugged me in return.

Neither of the two men had the slightest idea what her joke was about, but nevertheless in the spirit of "The Big Schmooze"—so they wouldn't lose points by appearing to be "out of the loop"—they joined in polite laughter.

Pleasantries attended to, Colleen took the lead by looking at me and saying, "We were just discussing the window treatment issues and Horatio had come up with a few really good ideas."

Thus ensued nearly twenty minutes of lively conversation about curtains and rods, drapes and sheers, shutters and blinds, and any and all combinations thereof—all between Colleen, Horatio and Bernard, with me standing by in mute attendance, valiantly trying to at least appear to be interested in what was being said.

About the time that Colleen, Horatio and Bernard were wrapping up, Weegee walked into the room.

By this time, I had drifted out of the main physical circle of conversation, so Weegee saw me first. And when he did, he hailed with, "Hey, Scuzman," smiling broadly.

Out of the corner of my eye I could see Horatio snicker at the appellation, and for that brief moment, I regretted Weegee and me being on such friendly terms. But I willed myself to get over the feeling and said, "Hey Weegee," in return and slapped him cordially on the back.

Horatio, I thought, *you're such a jerk.*

Then like Daniel into the lion's den . . . Weegee approached his mom and the two men.

"Weegee," his mother smiled warmly. "This is Mr. Blaire and Mr. Weston—Horatio and Bernard. They're going to help us decorate our home."

By this time I had begun to realize that to Bernard, the prospect of meeting anyone new, especially such a wild card as Weegee, did not make him comfortable. In fact, quite the opposite.

However, though obviously not relishing the experience of meeting Weegee, he looked as if he was going to make it, until the boy opened up with, "That's great. Hook and bait," and then leveled a steady gaze at both men.

Weston caved instantly, becoming a mere shadow of his former self, while Horatio, appraising Weegee in a somewhat predatory manner, smiled like the sharks do in cartoon shows and said, "Likewise, I'm sure."

For a second, as they say, you could have cut the silence with a Sawz-All.

It was Colleen who finally came to the rescue by saying, "Scott, why don't you and Horatio take a look at the office space in back while I go over some things with Bernard out here?"

And so we did . . . with Weegee remaining in the living room along with his mom and Bernard.

Damn. I would have given twenty bucks to watch Weegee continue to tee off on Weston if I could have. But duty called.

Alone now with Horatio, I asked casually, "So what's the relationship you and Bernard share? Are you partners in Weston Interiors?"

"We're not partners *per se*. It's a bit more symbiotic than that, if you know what I mean," Blaire answered glibly.

I didn't, but I figured he would get around to telling me if I gave him a little prompting.

"You mean, I scratch your back and you scratch mine?"

"In a manner of speaking . . . yes." Horatio surveyed me with his reptilian eyes. "Bernard's background is in interior design, mine is fine art."

"Oh, of course, the gallery. Does Mr . . . uh, Weston help you with that as well . . . in return, I mean?"

"My, but aren't we being formal," Horatio chided me snidely. "But yes, Mr. Weston does," rubbing it in a bit more.

Asshole.

"Not with the procurement of inventory or with artist relations, of course, but primarily by referring his clientele my way. There's an awful lot of wall space to fill in those Beverly Park barns. And we also furnish, well . . . How shall I put it? Other services as well," he added cryptically.

I wondered what he meant by that, but, suddenly remembering Smitty's skateboards, I found myself getting genuinely interested in the gallery itself.

"What's the name of your pla . . . gallery?" I asked

God. What was it about being around guys like this that always made me stumble and feel small—like my own very next breath didn't even belong to me, but to them?

"Ellipse. Do you like it?"

I was still mulling over my own question, but when I realized he was looking expectantly at me, I asked dully, "Like what?"

Stupid, stupid, stupid, I thought.

"The name, Ellipse." A tinge of exasperation in his voice now. "The Ellipse Gallery."

"Oh." And I commenced to think about it a bit.

Right off the bat, the word "Ellipse" conjured up patchy memories of complicated equations from my murky mathematical past. I knew what an ellipse looked like, of course, but at the time, back in school, the math had put me into a trance that I probably still hadn't fully recovered from.

But having said that, I was fairly certain that "deep forgetfulness" wasn't exactly what Blaire was going for in terms of an image to promote his gallery.

No. Hmmm . . .

Eliminating that option, my mind settled on a second, more likely alternative. That *Ellipse*—the sound of the word itself, without meaning or significance—actually had, in a somewhat vacuous way, sort of a slick, designer-like vibe to it.

Viewed in that light, the name probably did impart the exact aura of vague hipness, sophistication and flair that would appeal to the Westside moneyed set that Horatio was trying to woo.

Vacuouser and vacuouser.

"I like it," I lied.

"Or do you think Ellipses would be better?" Horatio pressed on.

"Is that with an *E* or a *Y*?"

"*E* or *Y*?" Blaire appeared perplexed at my question.

"You know," I clarified. "E-L-L-I-P-S-*E*-S or E-L-L-I-P-S-*Y-S?*" I regretted instantly that I had even brought it up.

"Don't be an idiot," Blaire berated. "With an *E*, of course."

I knew that was coming.

Then abruptly, dreamily reflective, he added, "Or, E-L-L-I-P-S-I-S-I-S . . . I've been toying with that the last couple of days as well," looking at me like he would suddenly value my opinion once again. What a charmer.

By this time, however, a childhood taunt had started to play inside my head . . .

"Yeah yeah-yeah *yeahhhh* yeah . . .
Don't care what you *call it*.
You're a stupid *poopy head* . . .
I'm not listening to *youuu.*"

"You know, Ellipse with the name Isis appended?" Horatio was looking at me expectantly.

Isis, I thought. *Hmmm* . . .

History had been even sketchier in school for me than advanced math.

Let's see, I thought . . . *Egyptian . . . mythological. A queen? Goddess? Both?*

"Why yes, of course," I finally managed.

"Yes, exactly." He gave me a knowing glance, and I gave him a fake one in return.

"Goddess-queen of the Nile," he rhapsodized, smiling dreamy-eyed again.

Exactly, I thought. She ought to fit right in with the crowd he was trying to attract—Isis, queen of denial and earnest self-delusion.

I was pondering this quirky factoid when I suddenly remembered Smitty's skateboards.

"Say, I know of an artist you might be interested in repping."

"Oh really, is he dead?"

"No."

"Terminal?" Hopeful.

"No."

"Third world?" His hope flagging. "You know, from some place war-torn or messed up—the son of a sexy drug lord, perhaps?" This last possibility noticeably appealing to him.

"He's from Fresno."

"Oh God . . . deliver us from Middle America." Blaire's eyes were appealing skyward, but then, suddenly hopeful again, "Is he . . . uh, open . . . uh, sexually, that is?"

"He's straight."

"Oh." Disappointed, but then, "An amputee . . . maybe lost a limb?" Getting a bit more desperate. "That always helps."

"*No,*" I said, disgusted.

"Blind?"

"How can any visual artist be blind?" I finally protested.

Horatio, irritated and dismissive now, said, "You're missing the point. He just doesn't sound like the kind of artist I could do anything with."

"How can you say that when you haven't even seen his stuff?"

"My dear boy." Patronizing, condescending now, Horatio declared, "Because he has no provenance, he has no . . . no back-story. What's his name?"

"Steve Smith."

Smugly triumphant, he went on, "You see? If someone doesn't even have enough imagination to come up with a more . . . more . . . ," searching for a satisfactory adjective, then blurting out, "artistic name . . . how the hell am I supposed to be able to do anything with him? How am I supposed to convince my clients that Joe Smith . . ."

"*Steve* Smith."

"Of course, Steve Smith from Oakland . . ."

"Fresno."

"Wherever!" Fury was in his eyes now. "How am I supposed to represent a guy as an artist . . . as someone different . . . as someone worthy of being . . . of being . . . of well, being worthy . . . if he's just a regular schmo? The answer is I can't." Menacing now. "And that's the truth about selling art, *Scuzman,*" he said, really putting a sneer into it.

"And even more to the point than that . . . ," he continued on a frothing roll, "if I, as a dealer . . . don't hold the line, don't act as a bouncer outside the glittering night club of civilized culture . . . ," Blaire paused a moment to admire his own metaphor, "and I just . . . uh . . . just let every Tom, Dick and *Steve Smith from Fresno* in, where would we be?

"Where would we be, indeed," he repeated rhetorically. "I'll tell you where we would be." He fixed me with a glare that could peel wallpaper. "We would all be hanging paint-by-number landscapes, or velvet Elvis portraits, or whatever Middle America hangs on their walls . . . on our walls.

"In short . . . the *WHOLE CIVILIZED WORLD AS WE KNOW IT* would go *RIGHT DOWN THE TUBES.*" This last sentiment delivered with such vehemence and violence directly into my face that for a short period—somewhat akin to the missing passages on the Nixon tapes—I knew not what transpired.

When my mental fog finally started to dissipate, I became aware of a distant voice, aggressive in tone. ". . . kind of game is he playing anyway? I mean, the kid's kind of a freak."

"Freak?" I inquired weakly, finally coming up for air.

"Yeah, Wedgy. That kid of hers." He motioned with his head toward the front of the house.

"You mean, Weegee . . . his nickname's Weegee," I said, somewhat defensively.

"Weegee, Wedgy, who gives a shit? The kid's weird. I mean, what is *That's great. Hook and bait* supposed to mean? Like I'm the hook and Bernie's the bait, or, or . . ." He contemplated all the various combinational possibilities, and coming up with nothing, finally gave up in disgust.

"*Dipshit.* The little monster's probably mental. Yeah . . . that's what it is." Horatio was liking the idea more and more, "The kid needs to be put on drugs. Fact is, everybody these days is crazy." Horatio went off on a generalized rant at this point. "Everybody . . . *everybody.*" Off into his "own little world" now.

Everybody, yeah right, I thought.

Blaire was looking more and more to me like a card-carrying psycho . . . or more appropriately, one who should be issued a card.

At this opportune moment, Colleen entered the room with Bernard in tow.

Weston looked a bit the worse for wear, no doubt from his extended exposure to Weegee.

That a boy.

"How are you two doing?" Colleen inquired cheerfully.

As if on cue, my cell phone rang. It was Nacho.

"Excuse me, Colleen, I've got to take this," I said, and I headed out of the room, leaving Colleen, Weston and Blaire to fend for themselves. "Hey Nacho, what's up?"

"*Como estás*, señor Scuz," Nacho responded enthusiastically. "We're installing the entertainment unit at Dale's place and . . ."

I tensed immediately, thinking, *God. Nothing wrong, please.*

". . . everything is going smoothly . . . we handled the TV thing and it was no *problema.*"

Thank you, Lord.

"Only thing is . . ." Again the shot of fear coursing through me. "He wants to add some more bookcase units along the hallway. Like to meet you out here today if possible 'cause he's returning to New York tomorrow."

Oh. A happy client . . . more work . . . more money . . . I could do that.

I looked at my watch. One-twenty-five.

"OK, Nach. I'm just about done here. I can be there in less than an hour."

That was going to cut things kind of close, traffic-wise, but it was all I could do.

After that, Nacho and I talked a little bit more about the job and then we both rang off.

By the time I got back to Colleen's future office, Colleen, Bernard and Horatio had left the room.

I finally found Colleen in the living room where she was just closing the front door, having evidently bid adieu to the two designers.

"That was fast," I said, genuinely surprised that the meeting had wrapped before it had really even begun. "I'm sorry . . . I could have put off my call if I'd known they had to leave immediately."

"Oh, don't worry about it, Scott." Colleen smiled a bit tiredly. "Bernard wasn't feeling too well and for some reason Horatio seemed a bit . . . preoccupied . . ." She was obviously a bit mystified herself at their sudden departure. "But . . . can I interest you in some lunch before Fabian arrives?" Colleen smiled, picking up the ball again.

"Fabian?" I quaked, losing any appetite I might have had.

"Yes, didn't Marney tell you? A designer named Fabian Mortenson also came highly recommended to me. He'll be here in forty-five minutes."

Well, shoot me in the ass and call me a raccoon.
Twice in one day.
I was dead meat.

Chapter Thirteen

A story set in Los Angeles could hardly be considered complete without at least a passing comment on the drivers, traffic, roads and freeways here.

Where do I begin? Let me start with Los Angeles itself.

The first thing someone who hasn't been to L.A. might notice upon arriving is how big, far-flung and spread out the whole affair is. In fact, L.A. is actually more of a location than it is a city.

"Greater L.A.," as it's sometimes referred to, is probably more than forty miles square if you take in everything from Pasadena, to Calabasas, Malibu down the coast to San Pedro and then back up the Harbor Freeway through South, Central and finally into "Downtown" Los Angeles, situated just west across the "river" from East L.A.

That's a lot of space. In fact, you could drop all of New York City into it and still have room enough for most of Chicago. Who's your Daddy now?

The purpose of the roads and freeways in L.A. is of course to tie all of these disparate areas together. No small task.

Now because L.A. is so big, you're going to spend about half of your time driving on streets and the other half on freeways. And boy, can traffic suck. Especially during rush hour.

Fortunately since I don't have to commute to work and can more or less set my appointments around the city at nonpeak traffic times, it's not so bad.

But even I've started to downgrade my optimism in this regard. I used to be able to count on getting anywhere in the city by freeway swiftly and easily between 10:00 A.M. and 2:00 P.M. But not anymore.

Now I don't know whether this is based on fact or is just a lingering impression of mine due to last spring's heavy rains and mudslides that closed down PCH and several of the canyons—wreaking major havoc with L.A.'s traffic in the process—but I'm obviously hoping it's the latter.

As far as street traffic goes, it's generally not as bad as the freeways.

There are a lot of cars, true, but about the only time things grind to a halt is when some selfish A-hole doesn't hold back on a yellow signal and winds up tying up the middle of the intersection for everybody else. However, for the most part, the streets are wide, clear and in good repair.

Aside from the freeway and surface street traffic here, there's also a relatively new mass-transit system composed of commuter trains, subway tunnels and, most recently, "The Orange Line" (or "Metro Line,"

I'm not exactly sure which), an express system featuring futuristic-looking double-car buses that for the most part travel along their own dedicated routes.

Having said this, however, I must confess that I know virtually nothing about it. For you see, to me, Los Angeles is and always has been a car town. In fact the cooler the car, the better.

Although possibly fifty years into the future this sentiment will characterize L.A.'s "before" mind-set, I just can't help it. And evidently, neither can the hundreds of thousands of other people out here on our highways and byways at any given time.

But beyond that, the factor that makes traffic even more unbearable than the quantity of drivers on the road in L.A. is the quality of them. Which brings me back to what I alluded to a few paragraphs ago: The primary cause of "bad traffic" in L.A. is bad drivers.

At the very top of my list of "bad" drivers are—you guessed it (or not)—Asians. Now I know that it's unfair for me to generalize and malign over half the population of the planet with this distinction, so let me revise that statement.

I feel the worst drivers in L.A. are (only) those Asians who are actually sitting behind the steering wheels of cars (trucks, buses, etc.), whether moving or not. There, that's a little more even-handed.

But taking this even a bit further, should my opinion in this matter still seem offensively groundless and false—though I personally feel that examples of my assertion are indeed legion—let me just say this: Skip it. You be your own judge, and let's just leave it at that.

My next worse driver category in L.A. is sort of a catch-all. I refer to this category as the "me first" driver.

However, "asshole" will also suffice. This is the driver that people most associate with "road rage" (either yours or theirs). Included in this category are the "arrogantly self-entitled" (mammoth SUV and luxury automobile drivers) and what I call the "aggressives."

In essence, the self-entitled driver type acts as if a dedicated street or freeway lane came included with their car as part of the price. They're also the ones who monopolize two parking spots in an overcrowded lot so as to safeguard their Porsche from door dings or, who, after pulling into a "handicapped" spot, vault from their convertible Lexus and sprint into Starbucks, leaving a blue wheelchair placard belonging to a distantly related and now deceased member of their family swinging breezily from their rear-view mirror.

The hallmark of the aggressive driver, on the other hand, is his or her propensity to constantly change lanes, tailgate and exceed speed limits—at least fifteen miles per hour above any posted limits, as opposed to the five to ten the rest of us are going.

Aside from more or less trying to lay sole proprietary claim to the roads and freeways here by weaving, speeding and tailgating in all lanes at all times, another favored haunt of the aggressive type is the right turn, or "parking lane" next to you at a stop sign. This is the position from which these drivers like to perform a cute little maneuver known as the "gutter sneak"—usurping said lane from what it was originally intended, and turning it into a "passing lane" of their very own. In this wise, they can shoot out ahead of everyone else the moment the light turns green.

Neat. I've actually seen this stunt pulled on the fly where, with the light having just turned green, the aggressive driver barreled up from the back of the pack somewhere, dodged to the right of all the cars waiting ahead of him or her at the signal and then punched it, merging back into traffic lanes and disappearing in a cloud of dust.

Gotta love 'em. In fact, come to think of it, stop lights and stop signs in general are a great location to spot aggressive drivers. But don't look for them to be stopped. They're the ones who aren't stopping. Enough.

The final bad driver type on my list is the "clueless" driver. For whatever reason, this type has relegated putting his or her attention on driving to a secondary priority. They include (but are not limited to) drunks, stoners, cell phone users, people who are so into music that they think they're in a club instead of a car, and those that choose to shave, apply makeup or read the newspaper while "driving."

However, there's one particular driver in the clueless category that warrants special mention: the overly "courteous" driver. This driver is a menace because they have such a fixation on "being nice" to their fellow motorists that they will routinely relinquish their right of way in a traffic encounter so as to "do for" another driver. This, of course, undermines any sense of prediction that anyone else might have regarding what the "courteous" driver is going to do next.

An instance comes to mind of one of these "drivers" slamming on their brakes to let some guy into the flow of traffic who was "stuck" off to the side of the road (poor guy), only to have this new addition, once in traffic, proceed to pull a T-turn and head in the opposite direction, tying up four lanes of cars, two in each direction, in the process.

Bottom-line message to "courteous" drivers: If you want to be nice to other people in cars, learn the basic rules of the road as well as the rules governing rights of way, and ABIDE BY THEM.

Secondly, if a stream of cars is FLOWING, do NOT do something strange or unexpected that will cause it to slow down, disperse or stop flowing altogether (as in the example just described). Otherwise, stay home and out of your car.

Having said all this, I would classify the vast remaining bulk of drivers in L.A. (about 80 percent, I would guess) as people who have, outwardly at least, the patience of Job and the benevolence of Mother Theresa.

Chapter Fourteen

I had left Colleen's place, declining her invitation to eat and greet and was now pulling into Dale Childs' estate in Pacific Palisades.

Dale is a very wealthy man of undeterminable financial provenance (at least to me). He never appears to "work" per se, but merely to talk on the phone periodically. I guess that's a nice gig if you can get it.

His rare book collection of the Samuel Johnson era is rumored to be worth more than his home, and his home is worth a bundle. With its 180-degree sweeping vista of the cool Pacific out front, to its secluded, tree-lined rear flank, he has what I would term quite an oasis—about fourteen acres worth. A staggering amount of land even by L.A.'s gold-coast standards.

I first met Childs when I was brought in to bid a library for his previous "temporary" digs in the flats of Beverly Hills, south of Sunset on Crescent Drive. The designer in charge of the project, Paul Forrest (who in his youth must have been a dead ringer for Paul McCartney) and I hit it off at our first meeting and I was hired for the substantial project on the spot, my previous work unseen.

The room came out great and Paul and I have stayed in touch, working on various projects for other financially well-endowed clients of his. When it came time for Dale to move to his current residence, Paul gave me the call.

As a side note here, I would like to say that Paul is one of the really good designers in L.A. He's probably pushing seventy but is still very professionally active, flying all over the world to attend to his high-end clientele.

He operates out of a beautiful Spanish-style apartment in Pasadena with the help of Mavis, his horsey-voiced secretary, and Janet, the latest in a long line of talented and bright assistants whom Paul, over the years, has hired, apprenticed and then eventually set free to pursue their own star.

I truly enjoy working with Paul, for it really is a collaborative activity and my only regrets—one present, one future—are that I didn't meet him years before I did and that I will not have spent as much time with him as I could have, when he is gone. A true artist, he is.

As I mentioned earlier, Fabian Mortenson is also involved in the current Childs project, but only in a peripheral way. You see, after Paul and I completed the design of the cabinets, Paul had to fly back east to oversee the renovation of a townhouse for some senator. That's when Mort got called into the picture.

Evidently, with Paul gone, Mrs. Childs had asked Mortenson to help her select the new carpets and drapes. And, prejudice on my part aside, Mortenson's actually quite good with that end of things.

As to exactly how the "wrong-sized TV" snafu came about, I could only guess that it had had something to do with "too many cooks." That is to say, Paul was gone, Mort was here, Mort had had a "second opinion" about the TV that Paul had selected—which, of course, Mort couldn't keep to himself—and the dominoes had just started tumbling from there.

Mort and I have crossed paths on various other projects that I've been involved with over the years and he's actually not that bad a guy, but, like I said, "too many cooks." So I was holding him at arm's length on this one, and hoping to keep him there.

"Scotty," Dale enthused, shaking my hand with his free right, still grasping a tennis racket with his left. "Nacho is doing his usual great job with the install and the design is very classy, if I may say so myself." He smiled broadly. "Care for a drink?" he asked.

Since Dale's DUI with the stripper last year and the moral compass correction his wife had urged upon him in its aftermath, I knew the only "drink" would be water, club soda or juice, which under other, merely parched circumstances, would have been fine.

"Thanks, no, Dale. I just had lunch," I fibbed.

"OK, well, let's look at what we've got going on in the hallway and then I'll let you and Nacho get together. I've got some more things I've got to take care of before I fly off to New York tomorrow."

Time is money, so they say. It was always the same story with the wealthier clients I worked with, but it never rubbed me the wrong way with Childs.

You see, for all his wealth and the social sway he could wield because of it, he had always been, to me at least, just a "regular guy." And that was much appreciated.

The "additional work in the hallway" that Nacho had told me Dale wanted turned out to be about thirty more linear feet of custom bookcases of the same design that we were installing in the media room. Which, I figured off the cuff, would be about four to six weeks more work for the shop. Nice.

"Just send my accountant, Fairaway, an invoice and he'll get you whatever money you need." Dale smiled and extended his hand. "Thanks for coming out, Scott." With that, he left to continue batting a little yellow ball around in the cool afternoon breeze.

You're welcome.

It was interesting the way that my business had evolved from at first making cabinets for neighbors in my parents' garage for not much money, to finally, twenty years later, "selling" four to six weeks worth of work with a handshake and a smile—for considerably much more. In fact, very interesting.

It's a maxim of successful business to be on the lookout for those factors that periodically create a sudden unanticipated increase in production, viability, etc. You know, you suddenly notice that green umbrellas are outselling red ones two to one, so you start stocking more green ones.

Today's "sale" was a perfect example. Something was definitely at work in the way that I conducted my business now that hadn't been present when I first started out.

I wasn't selling $40,000 worth of "extras" back then. I wasn't even selling $40,000 jobs. However, in spite of knowing this—that I should examine my business for these factors—I must admit that I was still hesitant to do so.

I think the reason for this, at least in part, was the fact that I'd always felt any success I'd ever had with my business had just one common thread: simply the fact that I enjoyed what I did and I cared to get it right.

I'd cared about what my clients wanted; I'd cared that they receive it; and I'd cared that the job was done correctly, whether the client "knew" what was going on technically or not.

And that didn't seem like such a significant "revelation."

Furthermore, the whole idea of running the business "more like a business" – maybe moving Nacho up to take over sales and grooming Rigo to head up the shop – sort of made me nervous too. It was hard for me to think of making changes like that no matter "how much more money or 'free time' I might have as a result." I mean, what next? Turn over designing cabinets too? What the hell would I do then?

Man, this was a classic example of the right thing to do feeling like the wrong thing to do. I could see that I was going to have to get hold of Maurice, the guy who helps me sort through things like this and see if we couldn't get to the bottom of it.

Then maybe one day I could take a vacation. You know, leave some guys in charge of things and not have to worry about my business disappearing while I was gone.

Speaking of guys in charge of things . . .

"Hey, Nacho," I said, "how's it going, my woodworking amigo?"

Chapter Fifteen

I should have known something was wrong with my truck when it labored up Sunset from PCH on my way to Dale's place, but instead, I knew it when it labored back down. Uh-ohh.

At least the meeting had gone well. Now I just had to figure out how I was going to get through the rest of my day without transportation, which in L.A., as I mentioned earlier, was going to be no small feat.

Big man about town, one minute. Big town about man, the next. Oh well. Triple-A to the rescue.

I could have had my truck towed north to Malibu, but since it was a holiday weekend and a nice south swell was running (good surf), it was unlikely that any mechanics I knew north of Topanga Canyon would be available to work on my truck until "after they'd finished the other projects they already had going." (Read: "after they'd surfed their brains out" or "after the swell dropped.")

Since the forecast was calling for wave size building up over the next couple of days, it didn't bode well for anything getting done on my truck in Malibu until next week.

Way too late. Consequently, I opted for a mechanic I know named Karl who has a little place on Lincoln Boulevard, close to the Marina.

The good news is he's not a surfer. The bad news, he's a boat mechanic.

As you may know, any product or service with the adjective "boat" or "marine" appended to it tends to cost twice as much as the same thing without. Even if it is the very same thing.

But Karl is very competent and I was "hoping"—just sort of going through the emotional motions, really—that the thousands of dollar bills I had herded his way over the years for repairing my boat would count for something.

I'd just have to spend tonight in the Marina, but hey, that might not be a bad idea, considering the run-in I'd had with Bernard and Horatio and then the bummer of my truck going south on me. That way I could catch a little R & R, maybe go for a sail. It wasn't even 4:00 yet.

If I was lucky, I might even get my truck back by noon tomorrow and be able to head back out to Paradise Cove to resume my vigilant sit at Ron's place before any potential burglars were any the wiser. It sounded like a plan.

After a few minutes under my hood, Karl gave an estimate of time and cost that proved me right with regard to both of my expectations. Yes, he could get the work completed by early tomorrow, and yes again, it was going to hurt.

I didn't know whether to feel good because I'd called it like it was or bad because it was like I had called it, so I decided to just give him my truck key and leave.

However, I did get a bit of a chuckle as I exited Karl's shop. A sign on the door leading out to the parking lot announced, "Feel free to fart." So I did.

Karl's place is about a mile from my boat as the gull flies and only about a mile and a half as the streets run, so I headed out on foot. As I sometimes do while walking, I started to think about stuff.

About a year after Shelly and I split, I bought my boat with the intention of living aboard and making it my home. But to my surprise, after only three months, I couldn't stand it anymore. As much as I loved staying on my boat for a day or two, I found that longer periods drove me batty.

It turned out I needed land under my feet in order to feel right. You know, with trees, houses and hills around me?

In essence, I found out that although I didn't like to live on the water or travel too far out in it, I liked to be near it. There's just something about the harmonious combination of the two elements, ocean and land, that soothes me.

But once I lose that balance—too much land and not enough ocean, or too much ocean and not enough land—it really bugs me.

Anyway, long story short, I wound up keeping my boat but looking for and settling into my current little apartment in Canoga Park. My place is in one of those "garden apartment" complexes you read about in sunny rental brochures that, according to my experience prior to my current situation, can be somewhat hit-or-miss with regard to the "garden."

However, in the case of my place, the developer actually did a very nice job. Even though there are probably well over a hundred units in the complex, there are plenty of trees and shrubbery, the patios are private and the general vibe and views are green and peaceful.

My little place is so nice, in fact, that in my opinion, I have the best of both worlds: a cozy apartment in the "woods" and a "beach house" on the water. Not bad.

As I mentioned earlier, I lived in the shop for about six months after my divorce and at that time I thought about buying a house in the Valley, but I never did. The main reason being that I couldn't find any place that I liked. Really liked.

Given the amount that real estate prices have shot up since then, maybe I should have bought something. Anything. But then there was the fact of me having grown up at the beach that wouldn't let me do it—wouldn't let me buy something "inland."

Of course, besides the Valley, I looked in Santa Monica, looked in Venice, and once, in dreamy desperation, up toward the southern end of Malibu. But I didn't find anything I could afford that rang any bells.

Then one day on a disrelated whim, I walked into Catalina Yachts in Marina del Rey where Doug Pace showed me *Simple Pleasures*, a twenty-eight-foot sailboat. The price was reasonable, only about 10 percent of even the crumbiest house I'd looked at up to that point, and I couldn't beat the "on the water" location (or so I thought at the time). Doug said he would even throw in the "slip" (the parking spot where a boat is moored) if I bought her, so I signed the papers that day.

There's enough room inside for me to stand up comfortably, which in my case was a must, and the boat is very "beamy" (wide) so the kitchenette, bathroom, bedroom and living room are very spacious and comfortable for a boat its size.

I keep an extra set of clothes, some books, a computer with a DVD player, and a guitar on board. I've also got a bike in storage nearby. This way I'm set for a night or two if I want to plan a getaway from the Valley's summer heat or, like in this case, wind up having to stay here on the spur of the moment.

Catalina Yachts has a great anchorage, set way back into the harbor as far from the coast as possible. True, the docks themselves are a bit old. But the slips are very affordable and Paul, the office manager, is a good guy and an excellent sailor to boot.

As far as local attractions and amenities go, my current favorite restaurant is Tony P's. It's actually a major sports bar—which I'm not particularly into—but it also has a room for quiet dining, as well as a separate enclosed deck area overlooking the boats outside. That's where I always sit.

The menu is varied and the food is surprisingly tasty, well prepared and very reasonably priced. I love the "wedge salad" – a near quarter head of iceberg lettuce covered with dressing and diced tomato bits. That, with a beer or two, is often all I'll get.

Another local attraction for me is the Marina's public library, which is right on the water, quite literally 500 feet from my boat. They've got a great selection of art books, and sometimes I just drop in for a browse.

It was my mother who first got me into going to the library when I was a kid of maybe eight or nine. I guess it made a lasting impression on me because I've stuck with it over the years.

I remember Saturday afternoons spent with her at the Fullerton Public Library over near Hillcrest Park—me in my section reading *The Hardy Boys*, *Nancy Drew* (I'm man enough to admit it now), *The Adventures of Miss Pickerell*, *Danny Dunn and the Homework Machine* and all those fabulous children-sized biographies in their neat orange bindings; and Mom in hers, somewhere off in the "Grownup" section.

Although I know she loved to take me there—for I know she loved to go herself—she never said so in so many words. It was all very light-touch, her introducing me to the library. No forcing me to go, or "it's good for you" lectures.

After all, what kid wants to do what's "good" when he can do what's fun? In fact, now as I look at it, I guess that was her "strategy."

She made it fun for me—gradually, of course—the experience peppered liberally with trips to the nearby park and Baskin Robbins ice cream on the way home, until, eventually, going to the library itself became fun. That was quite a masterful trick to successfully pull off with a rambunctious eight-year-old boy.

My most vivid sense memory of those library visits was the quietude. How the sheer volume of the books throughout the "great room," where I mainly read, acted as a dampening agent to any sound that somehow suddenly introduced itself upon the otherwise pleasantly hushed environment.

A dropped book, a sneeze, the twitter and rustle of young girls sharing gossip so intoxicating that it got away from them for a moment. All violating, of course, the cardinal rule of the room: *SILENCE!* But then, just as suddenly as each would intrude, they would be absorbed back into the most satisfyingly tranquil peace I think I have ever enjoyed.

At the time, I thought all mothers brought their kids to the library. Looking back on it now, however, boy, was I mistaken.

In truth, I had the very rare good fortune of being brought up by an extraordinarily special person who cared a great deal about me and the power and value of reading. So, almost thirty years after the fact, I would like to say*, Thanks, Mom.*

I guess, in part, this is why I'm so high on looking words up in the dictionary. In fact, now more than ever.

You see, in these times of catchy sales slogans and political sound bites, of twenty-word pitches, and of unscrupulous men who use them to manipulate those among us who are already too far gone to understand anything else, there is still an element of our language that is impervious to "spin," "rhetoric" and "double-speak": the definition of words. For as humble as these foot soldiers of the language may seem, they are yet the building blocks of virtually all there is that can be known and communicated.

Master the words and you can master the world. At least, that's my motto.

For there is no phrase, speech, book or subject that will not surrender before them, nor confusion, lie or misconception that can survive for long in the light of their understanding.

Amen.

Now let's see what else is of interest to me in the Marina that I'd like to relate at this time. *Hmmm . . .*

Oh . . . from the sublime to the mundane.

The twenty-four-hour supermarket a block from my boat has been torn down for about a year now. However, I was over at the shopping center it anchors the other day.

What a shock. As I described early on in this book, the Marina has always had sort of a funky beach vibe that I have always found very refreshing. But if what I saw on my little visit the other day is any indication of things to come, those funky days are over, Rover.

Beemers, baubles, poodles and pretense. I felt like one of the Beverly Hillbillies as I wound my pickup truck 'round and 'round the parking lot, searching in vain for a place to park. OK, "poodles" is a bit of a stretch, but you get what I mean.

Granted, now there's a Starbucks, which is a very welcome replacement for the place that used to sell "coffee" with a vaguely petroleum-like taste and sheen to it—a residue from some product the purveyor used to clean the coffee maker with, perhaps? I never knew and never wanted to know. God, that swill was awful.

The health food market-cum-restaurant is still going strong and even Chipotle, the burrito place, has a pleasantly upgraded look, which is great on both counts.

West Marine, of course, still anchors the south end of the lot. Though taken more these days for a clothing store with a "nautical theme" by the seemingly swelling-by-the-day masses of tourists that frequent the area, it's still the "go to" supplier for the local boat people.

And even the Ralphs, which over the years had become rather dowdy, mildewy and tired, now looks like something out of an epicurean wet dream. Very inviting and nice.

So what's my beef?

Oh, I don't know. I guess the thing that really got me going about the center's "new look" was just mainly one new addition.

A snooty-looking jewelry store.

Come on. This is Marina del Rey, not Monte Carlo.

That, and the new parking arrangement that seemed too much to me like one of those endlessly serpentine lines for the Matterhorn at Disneyland. I mean, *What the heck.* I got so upset that I fled the scene without buying, or even being able to remember what I had gone shopping for there in the first place.

You see, between one thing and another—going out of town for a few weeks and then being over-the-top busy with my business for the next three months after I returned—I had kind of lost track of what had been going on with the center's renovation. Then one day I returned to buy an avocado sandwich (that's what it was) and . . .

WHAM! It hit me. The place was different. So much so, in fact, that it had sort of shaken my sense of "life continuity," if you know what I mean. And it was going to take me some time to get used to it.

Fortunately, by the time I had reached this nadir of thought, I had also reached my boat.

Ah, *Simple Pleasures.* My stress lifted and blew out to sea.

Chapter Sixteen

"Scuz."

It was Smitty. He had evidently been skateboarding a circuit of the Marina and spotted me on my boat, so I walked up to the top of the dock ramp and opened the gate.

"*Cómo estás*?" I smiled and held the gate for him to walk through.

"*Com ce, com ca*," he responded with a yawn. "Today is a holiday so I've just been kickin' it."

Holiday? I thought. Labor Day wasn't for three days.

Hmmm . . . It's not a national, at least not an American national. Foreign?

Oh hell, who was I trying to kid? I wouldn't be able to figure this out if there were money riding on it.

"Carriage Day." Steve smiled smugly as he dropped his skateboard to its wheels, sprang onto its back and shot all the way down the ramp and out onto the dock twenty feet below.

Carriage Day?

"I've never heard of it. What the hell kind of holiday is that?" I called out, following him down.

"First off, what difference would it make whether you'd heard of a holiday or not?" said Smitty, fixing me with a mildly accusatory glare. "It would still exist."

"Yeah, but if I didn't know it existed, I wouldn't celebrate it—neither would anybody else," I argued up a slope of logic that I knew from experience was becoming slipperier by the moment.

"Precisely," he responded, coolly triumphant. "That's why I've made it my business to research this area and compile a complete database on the subject," he said as he began to spin his skateboard on the tip of his index finger, the way some basketball players do a ball.

God, I thought, *it's both mesmerizing and annoying to get into conversations with him like this.*

"You see, if you really think about it . . . ," Steve went on, now transferring the still spinning skateboard behind his back to his other index finger.

How the hell did he do that?

"On any given day of the year, there's a holiday of some sort. Granted," shooting me a concessionary glance, "some are kind of marginal, like Interception Day." Putting his attention back on his still spinning board, "But that only comes around every six years."

Was he kidding?

"But a holiday like Carriage Day, well, that's got a respectable third-tier rating."

Third tier?

"Now, above the third tier, you've got your second tier. You know, Secretaries' Day." Fanning his board faster and faster, "Government Employees' Day." Smitty suddenly frowned. “Right . . . ,” he muttered sarcastically to himself, “like they need another day off. Dipshits,” flipping the spinning board mid-expletive from his left index finger back to his right, as if to underscore his contempt.

Once he’d cooled off a bit, he continued, “Anyway, they’re second tier and there’s about fifty of them,” fanning the board back up to speed. “But moving on up to first tier, of course, you’ve got your Christmas, Hanukkah, Ramadan, MLK and Kwanzaah. Important days like that.” Admiring the board now, spinning in a blur, “All in all, about fifteen to twenty more of them.

“By the way,” he suddenly interjected, “you’re into words,” flicking his attention on me for a moment. “Did you know that the word ‘holiday’ comes from Old English, meaning ‘holy day’? Neat, huh?”

Without waiting for any response from me, he resumed watching his spinning board wind down to nothing until at last it just stood there, balancing on his outstretched finger.

Positively neat-o keen-o, I thought.

“Like I said,” he finally continued, letting the board fall into his open hands to emphasize the point, “below these first two tiers are all the third-tier holidays. And there’s hundreds of them.” Working the board up and around to the back of his neck now, “So many in fact, that on any given day, there’s something going on, somewhere.” He smiled and winked conspiratorially at me. “You just have to be attuned.”

With that, he started using one of the knobby bolts on the bottom of the board to scratch an itch that had evidently developed between his shoulder blades.

"Yeah. Yeah. *Yeah,*" he wriggled his back against the bolt as if he was having an orgasm. *"Attuuuuuunnnnnned,"* his whole upper body shuddering with pleasure until, at last, his eyes closed and a blissfully peaceful expression infused his face.

"Know what I mean?" he finally asked, his eyes opening. With that, he let the skateboard drop to his side, its tail coming to rest on the dock.

"Uh . . . er . . . uh . . . ," I strove to respond.

"Yeah." He cut me off, smiling. "Say no more, *compadre.*"

Brother, he had no cause for concern on that account.

"I can tell," he said, "we're *simpatico* on this one."

With that, his shoulders drooped, his whole body went slack, and he just stood there looking at me for what seemed like ten seconds. At last a slight agitation gripped his face and small lines started etching around his eyes.

"Got any food?"

He was "back."

"No, Smitty. I can't say that I do, because I don't," I replied, slipping into a Jimmy Stewart drawl that suddenly seemed appropriate to the situation.

"Downer," his eyes moving now in a vague, distracted way—up over my shoulder (at a seagull?), out to a sailboat in the harbor, darting over toward Lincoln Boulevard and then finally back in my general direction.

"Got any beer?"

Well, as it turned out, I did. And within an hour, Smitty and I had drunk it all—five or six beers apiece—on empty stomachs. Then we fell asleep.

The nagging ring of my cell phone dragged me out of my stupor and into the realization that the dream I had been having about someone belt-sanding my cheek had been "inspired" by me passing out, face down, on the knobby-tufted material that encases the settee cushions in my boat like the skin of a crocodile—waterproof, mildew-proof, stain-proof and comfort-proof.

"Lo?" I croaked.

"Scuz? What's wrong?" It was Marney. Mild urgency in her voice.

Why is it that women always want to know "what's wrong"? I bridled at the notion. I mean, I'd just gotten on the phone, for Christ's sake.

"Nothin'," I said, imbuing my answer with just a hint of "surprise" at her asking, scrambling now to find my watch that had somehow fallen from my wrist.

Inclination to daytime inebriation isn't a trait I admire in myself. It was still daytime, wasn't it?

"I uh . . . was uh . . . just going over some stain samples with my guy down here in the Marina," relieved at hitting on something semiplausible right out of the gate. However, suddenly realizing my "explanation" hadn't explained much, I hastily elaborated, "The stuff's pretty gnarly." Then, rushing to clarify, yet again, "The chemicals, I mean."

GOD.

"Oh . . . You sounded like you were drunk."

SHIT. OK, at this point I've got to admit something about women that you, the men reading this book, can take to the bank. Truth be told, when it comes to suspecting what's going on with men, most women are pretty much right on the money, most of the time.

Now, in fairness, it could be argued on the flip-side that this is because men, for the most part, are fairly predictable creatures. However, no matter which side of the argument you come down on, the fact remains that since so-called "women's intuition" is still only a suspicion (in my biased opinion), Marney, like most all women—wanting to believe, wanting to console, wanting to comfort—can eventually be "sweet-talked" out of almost anything if the man involved can keep his mouth shut long enough to allow the woman to accomplish it herself.

So at this point, I fell completely silent and just waited.

At length, concern starting to seep into her voice, Marney asked, "You are OK, aren't you?"

"Yeah," I said, taking my time to reply. "It's just that . . . well, you know . . . (Blah, blah, blah)."

As my friend Swifty Fry puts it, "If you can't blind women with brilliance, baffle them with bullshit."

Oh, *come on.*

I can feel a backflow of animosity from some of you female readers now. I mean, what do you expect a man to do in response to the question, "What's wrong?"?

Confess? "Confess" what? It's almost like men are forced into lying by women who follow them around all the time, asking, "What's wrong?".

How about asking, "What's right?" for a change? That would be a good question to ask. You know, "What's right, honey?" Then everybody would feel good. Because it's the needless lying about needless things that drags everyone down—makes everybody feel bad. And that's how I was feeling about Marney right now.

It wasn't even like drinking a few beers was such a big deal, but it still bothered me. It worked and it wormed and it made me feel like a louse. I mean, such a trivial, little, insignificant, unimportant thing. But in the end, I had lied about it, and that fact gnawed at me like a rat on a rope.

Damn. Whatever happened to that sappy movie sentiment, "Love is never having to say you're sorry"? Didn't that hold water anymore? Probably not, I guessed, because if the way I was feeling was any indication, the likelihood of an apology-free future didn't look too promising. Oh well.

When I finally got off the phone, Steve, who had apparently woken up about halfway through our conversation, blurted out, "So what's the deal? Who's Marney and where's the party?"

"She's uh . . . ," I began wearily, and then caught him up on everything that Marney and I had been through over the last thirty-six hours.

Or, almost everything.

"And yeah, we've been invited to a reception for a couple of artists up in Beverly Park, at the home of some collectors. An artist named Karizma?" I looked questioningly at Smith. "And another named Pole?"

"Pole. Hmmm . . ." Steve thought about the name, "Doesn't sound familiar. But, Karizma . . ." Brightening up, "Yeah. I've seen her handbills up and down Abbott Kinney. Shows her stuff at Johnny B Wood from time to time."

"Yeah?" I said, surprised. "I thought John was into retro furniture."

"Maybe he's branching out," Smitty reasoned. "But this Karizma," getting back to his main interest in the conversation, "she's a real looker—at least from what I could see outside the trash can." At this, Steve smiled and drifted off into thought.

"Trash can?"

"Yeah," said Smitty, returning to the here and now. "On her handbill. Shows her standing waist-deep naked in a trash can, holding a couple of cantaloupe rinds over her boobs. Really kind of . . . well, trashy, if you'll pardon the pun. But hot, real hot. As a matter of fact . . . ," his eyes lit up, remembering. "Here she is!" He removed a piece of paper from his back pocket and passed it to me.

I unfolded the neon green handbill and looked in shock at the eyes of the young woman who was staring back at me. Time seemed to collapse and I could almost taste the droplets of sweet fruit juice that trickled down her abdomen.

"See what I mean?" Steve leered.

God, I sure did. Only too well.

So much so, in fact, that I didn't know whether to look forward or backward to seeing her tonight.

Damn. How the hell did this happen? I asked myself, not expecting, nor really wanting an answer, ever. Suddenly I felt antsy, dirty and irritated all over.

"Let's get the hell out of here, Steve," I blurted as I headed topside.

"I thought you said your truck was in the shop."

"No, I mean let's go for a sail. This whole day has gone sideways on me and I just need to get some space—straighten some things out. What do you say?"

"I'm for it if you don't mind me going for a couple of burritos while you get things rigged."

I didn't, and he split.

By the time he was back, *Simple Pleasures* was ready to go.

The prevailing wind in Marina del Rey is from the southwest and blows directly into the open end of my slip. Because of this, I like to moor my boat facing into it so I can just sail right out, instead of using the motor.

It's riskier with a boat this size, but a lot more fun. In fact, the moments just prior to sailing my boat out of the slip never cease to conjure up the exact same feeling in me: that somehow she, still fettered to the dock but fully rigged, her sails snapping, popping and yearning to be filled, is excited and alive in the same way that a horse must be at the starting gate of a race—pawing, snorting and growing more charged by the second at the prospect of running free.

And when the moment does arrive and the final restraints are loosed, the slightest urging on my part of "Let's go, girl" is all it requires and she takes off flying. It's an exhilarating relationship to be part of and it always gets me stoked.

The wind was blowing about ten knots as Smitty and I sailed up and out of the harbor and continued west across the Santa Monica Bay toward Topanga Canyon—out to where the late afternoon sun was heading. The breeze was steady and clean, the sun, simple and warm, and the swell was relatively mild. And the burritos that Steve had bought tasted better than the sum of their parts.

In short, we had both settled into a very relaxed mood by the time we had returned to the dock and cleaned up the boat.

Chapter Seventeen

"I don't know, I've been thinking about getting one too," I said over my shoulder to Smith in the back seat of Marney's Beetle.

The top was down and the warm evening breeze was wafting all around us as we headed up Laurel Canyon, toward Mulholland.

"I'm telling you, man, it's a chick's car," Steve responded adamantly. "No guy who's straight is going to be caught dead owning a VW Beetle. I don't care how many hippies owned them back in the day."

"Oh come on, Steve," said Marney, having just met him but evidently taking a liking to his feisty off-center persona already. "They're cute."

"That's my point. Any guy who drives one of these things is going to be taken for a wuss. And last I knew, that wasn't exactly the kind of image Scuz was trying to cultivate. He's already waist deep in homo clients, for Christ's sake. Get a MINI, dude."

"Yeah, they're cool," I said. "But, I think they might just be a little too cool. You know the whole Beemer thing? Besides, there doesn't seem to be as much room in a MINI as there is in a Beetle."

"First of all," Smitty, winding up again, "too cool? That's not possible. And room around your ass? That's the last thing you're going to be concerned about, you get a bug." He was giggling to himself.

"Yeah, well, all I know is I've got to find something that gets better gas mileage than my truck. I'm getting tired of bending over every time I go to the gas station."

"Thats what I'm talking about. Bending over? You don't know bending over, dude. You think you do, but you buy a Beetle and you're going to be on a whole new first-name basis with it. For real." Laughing now, "Up close and very personal. Like with a guy named Raoul, or Timmy, or Troy. Might as well place a GWM personal in the *L.A. Weekly*."

"GWM?" Marney asked.

"Gay, white, male."

Marney was laughing now, too. "That ad ought to really pull."

"Yeah, pull his pud. But try and tell this moron. He's so . . . so . . . theoretical about everything—like reality is optional with him. No wonder he's so wayward."

"Wayward?" I stepped back into the fray. "Look who's talking. You're about as optional and wayward as anyone I know and I know plenty of optional and wayward, believe me."

"All I'm saying is," Steve launched into his summation, "you've got to regulate a little in life. You can't just go off too heavy in one direction. Buy a bug?" he wailed. "I think you've already got enough warm and sensitive in your life without going way out of whack buying a chick's car too. VW?" snorting in disdain

"Get a Mustang—five-speed stick; three hundred and twenty-five horses; black with red leather interior. To hell with the mileage. I mean, who cares? This is L.A.." And with that, Smitty slumped down into the back seat in silence.

Well, I had to admit, he was right about one thing . . . This was L.A. Whatever that meant.

But as far as my buying a Beetle was concerned, I was going to have to get a second opinion. Because the problem was . . . In spite of all that Smitty had said—and I couldn't help agreeing with him to a certain extent—I liked 'em.

I just couldn't help myself. So where did that leave me?

I guess for starters, I'd have to find three or four more guys—you know, *guy* guys—but not as over-the-top as Smitty. Ones who could help me fend off the inevitable feeling that Steve was right about the Beetle being a chick's car.

But where was I going to find them? I didn't have a clue. Shit.

As I mentioned earlier, Beverly Park is a swanky enclave of homes in a Disneyland-like setting off Mulholland between Coldwater Canyon and Benedict Canyon. Although I've been involved with a couple of projects there over the years, for the most part they're out of my league.

Not because of the quality of the work, but because of the quantity.

I'm talking huge houses with truckloads of cabinetry, miles of moulding and tons of custom detailing—you know, grand staircases, hidden bookcase panels, carvings, and just lots of wild stuff in general.

I remember one place that I worked on had a master closet for the "lady of the house" that went on and on for about 100 feet. We supplied some of the custom mouldings for it. It came out beautifully, but it took an army of guys to bring it in on schedule—not just our shop.

Just then, Marney pulled up to the little guardhouse at the Mulholland entrance of Beverly Park.

"Yes, we're with the Weston-Blaire reception," I heard her tell the guard.

God, I thought, *just the names of those two guys put me on edge.*

I'd really gotten a bad feeling from both of them at Colleen's today and my opinion hadn't improved with time. I sure hoped Marney knew what she was getting into.

She'd told me on the phone this afternoon that Horatio had taken an interest in her painting—thought her coming to tonight's reception would be a good way for her to, in his words, "get a better idea of the way the art scene works."

How the hell did that happen so fast? I wondered.

Maybe he felt the name Marney was more "artistic" than Steve Smith.

Come on, Scuz, I thought, *don't get wacked out cynical so fast. Give the situation a chance.*

OK, how about fat chance? Ah, hell. No matter how objective I tried to be, I still had a bad feeling about it. A real bad feeling.

Speaking of "bad feelings"—and isn't that the way negativity tends to go, one downer thought leading to another?—I almost died when Smitty showed me that handbill of Karizma. What the hell was that all about?

On one hand, I didn't want to know. But on the other . . . Well, let's just say, I didn't feel confident I'd be able to avoid it.

Man, this was shaping up to be one heck of a night. I hoped they had an open bar.

When the guard at last waved us through and we started down the gentle incline toward the softly sweeping gate, I couldn't help having the exact same feeling I get when embarking on a roller coaster ride that I didn't really want to go on in the first place: *Will this be the last thing I ever do?*

I know that may seem a bit melodramatic, but I'm not a roller-coaster type of guy. I like to feel in control of my own destiny, and if I'm going to suffer, I want it to be while doing something worthwhile—not while doing something frivolous and dumb like pulling eight G's in an "amusement" contraption, or, and more to the immediate point, from getting involved with a guy like Horatio Blaire, if I could avoid it.

Oh well. I was too late for second thoughts.

Immediately upon making the first "S" turn below the gates and emerging out of the shadow of the tall line of shrubbery that formed a sonic barrier between Mulholland and the inside of the park, we were all—individually and collectively—relieved of any further need to wonder whether we'd be able to find the house where the reception was being held.

For rolling up along the pleasant roadway that beckoned before us—in fact, careening off the façade of every structure in its path—came a howling, demonized cacophony of sound, like five dozen Marshall amps of heavy-metal yore, frying on steroids.

"*Luuuv!* (two, three, four, one, two)
Bitch-slap, *Luuuv!* (two, three, four, one, two)
Talkin' 'bout *Luuuv!* (two, three, four, one, two)
Bitch-slap, *Luuuv!* (two, three, four, one, two)"

Catchy.

Whoever was hosting this little shindig wasn't the shy and retiring type. On top of that, they had to be loaded to induce their neighbors to turn a deaf ear to what was going on. Maybe they were all down in their wine cellars, or their bowling alleys, drunk, with earmuffs on.

And to think that I'd thought this was going to be a quiet affair—shrimp cocktail, champagne and a jazz combo. Man, was *I* out of touch.

"My God," Smitty said, his voice somehow cutting through the aural onslaught. "It's the Cumbers," his eyes taking on a look of fevered excitement.

"The *WHAAAAAT*?" I screamed at the top of my lungs, my words bounding off down the little valley before us like a yodel into a canyon.

For, you see, at the very instant I unleashed my query, the "music" stopped, creating a veritable vacuum of vibration save for the sound of my own voice, now ricocheting from manse to manse all around the otherwise completely quiet neighborhood.

"Cooool." Smitty eyed me admiringly. "You've got quite a set of pipes. You ever think about being a singer? You wouldn't even need a microphone."

"Thanks," I rasped, trying to swallow my vocal chords back to where they belonged. "What did you say?"

"I said you can really belt it out," Steve answered. "You ought to—" But I cut him off mid-sentence.

"No, before that. You said, The Bummers?"

"Bummers? Oh . . . The Cumbers. Yeah, that's what I was saying. That band sounds like The Cumbers," Steve said, beaming excitedly once more.

"What kind of name is The Cumbers?" Marney asked.

"It's actually The Cucumbers. But over time, unlike their reputation," Smitty explained, fidgeting impatiently like a gossip with some fresh dirt he couldn't wait to dispense, "they shortened it to The Cumbers."

"Since when did rockers resume foraging through the vegetable kingdom for band names?" I asked, more out of annoyance than interest. "I thought that went out in the sixties with The Kadota Figs."

"That's what I'm trying to tell you," Smitty whined with excitement. "The inspiration for their name wasn't so much botanical . . . ," Steve at first fixing me with a slyly leerful look, but when he saw I wasn't paying attention, turned it on Marney, "as anatomical."

It took a couple of seconds, but the penny dropped. And Marney's face, even in the faint glow of a nearby streetlight, turned discernibly crimson.

Then, it dropped for me too.

"Classy," was all I could manage. "Real classy."

"It . . . it sure is brazen," Marney volunteered gamely, trying not to appear as embarrassed as she was. "Really in your face."

"You better believe it," Smitty crowed. "They're—"

"DON'T," I interjected, "go there, Smitty."

He just giggled.

Chapter Eighteen

By the time Marney's car had been valeted and we finally walked "into" the actual party, a white rapper was holding forth on a little stage above the horseshoe drive abutting the cozy 40,000-square-foot main house. A portable dance floor had been laid out on the driveway in front of him and a few dozen people were working out their frustrations on one another.

Out on the front lawn between the two legs of the driveway, a huge open-sided tent had been erected and lit up to serve as an art gallery on one side and a bar on the other. On the gallery side, forty or more pieces of art hung from wires strung up into the tent's vaulted ceiling, while on the bar side, guests milled around, attended by liveried servants, the hors d'oeuvres and liquor flowing.

Off the driveway leg farthest from the house, a narrow service drive meandered out past a dense stand of trees where it terminated at a twelve-car "stable," complete with its own gas pump and service garage. Some kids with "rice rockets"—souped-up Japanese street racers like those featured in the movie, *The Fast and the Furious*—were doing burnouts on the cobbled drive in front of the garages.

In short, if one subscribed to the notion that "anything worth doing is worth overdoing," this party had gotten off to a rollicking good start.

However, if one did not—like yours truly—it was sensory overload at first sight. For this and the couple of other reasons that I enumerated previously, I announced to no one in particular, "I need a drink," and headed off solo toward the bar.

I don't know whether it's the fact that my dad used to drink gin when I was a kid and I grew accustomed to and eventually liked its smell, or whether I just developed an affinity for it on my own. But the fact remains, it's my "hard drink" of choice. So, I ordered a triple with tonic water and ice from a bartender done up in a white powdered wig and a purple waistcoat.

In these proportions the gin was a bit overpowering, like a whiff of the jet fuel that I sometimes inhale at Nacho's shop, so I made a mental note to return for more tonic water once I drank the glass down a bit—if I didn't "forget."

Marney had joined Steve in walking over toward the stage and since I didn't want to get into a confrontation with her about the gin—I imagined she could probably smell it from a few feet away—I headed toward the gallery.

It wasn't until about five years ago that I finally "got" galleries and museums, or more correctly, art on display in galleries and museums. Before that it was more about how I felt I "should" respond to the pieces on display, rather than how I was responding to them.

And I can explain the thing that changed my appreciation of art in one word: FREEDOM.

You see, I finally realized that that was what art was all about for me: what an artist had "pulled off" or "gotten away with" despite all the reasons that he or she shouldn't have been able to. Like a composer artfully improvising his way out of a musical "dead end"; an architect seamlessly blending an esthetic structure with a beautiful but difficult site; a sculptor achieving the illusion of weightlessness with a two-ton block of stone; or a writer sending thoughts and emotions winging through space and time by encoding them into words on a page.

In short, it's an artist's courage, ingenuity, determination, skill and grace at communicating a message—at getting something through to someone else, despite the adversities of his or her own chosen medium—that I find the most fascinating thing about art.

Their triumphs, manifest in their completed creations, inspire me with the possibility and hope of achieving my own triumphs and freedom. Now that's what I dig about art.

As I got closer to the gallery tent, I could see that the hanging space was equally apportioned for the two artists, Karizma and Pole (Tad Pole? Pole Cat?)—room for about twenty pieces each.

Since the open-sided tent afforded no wall space of its own, the framed works were suspended from the tent's ceiling in pairs—back-to-back, one side for Karizma, the reverse side for Pole. In this way, two meandering viewing paths were created with the artworks themselves, forming the "walls" of the lanes.

I'm no expert on gallery arrangement or lighting, but the pieces seemed very well presented and the overall effect quite pleasing.

I entered Pole's viewing path first.

What can I say?

The old observation that "beauty is in the eye of the beholder" came to mind. But in reverse.

For in the case of Pole's first offering, a vigorous black-and-white (in more ways than one) self-portrait photograph entitled "Pole Dance," I was holding no beauty for it and it was echoing the same.

Although I was beginning to understand the derivation of his nickname, I wasn't sure why someone would want to pay for, or, as in my case, even get a free visual explanation of it.

Nevertheless, I continued to the next photograph . . . and the next . . . and the next, all in quickening succession.

Unfortunately "North Pole," "South Pole" and, finally, "Polar Bare" (sic) were all variations along the same "veins," so to speak.

"Ah, hell," I said at last, and took a two-finger slug of my G & T.

When I came up for air, I was surprised to hear a small female voice at about 4:00 o'clock (navigational term, meaning slightly behind my right side).

"Mesmerizing, aren't they?"

I turned through the haze that the gin had begun to cast and was surprised to see a little old lady in freshly lacquered red hair, a long-sleeved country-and-western shirt and tight designer jeans tucked into the tops of a pair of blue cowboy boots.

I don't know if it was the gin, the persisting mental images of Pole, or the vision of her that struck me speechless, but I couldn't for the life of me frame a response to her question. So I just gave her a wink and a knowing (for a drunk guy) grin.

"I've been through this exhibit over and over, all night long," she continued, undeterred by my lack of comment, "and all I can say is . . . it's just so inspiring. It makes me feel so . . . so free."

Boy, I wasn't expecting that.

"Free, that's what it is," she added, wrenching her attention from Pole's photograph to face me directly and grabbing my right arm—the one with my drink at the end of it—with her surprisingly strong left hand.

All I could do was look at her, then longingly at my gin and then back at her again.

"I simply must meet Mr. Pole," she blurted as if she thought I might be able to help her accomplish that. "When Bob and Dorothy told me they were having a reception for a couple of young artists, I had no idea their themes would be so . . . so universal."

At last correctly reading my lack of response as complete shock—I was by this time sobering up, but not quite fast enough—the woman moved to at least partially rectify the matter.

"Oh how impolite of me," she smiled sweetly. "I'm Virginia Mathews, Bo and Do's neighbor." (Pronounced "Bow," as in bow and arrow, and "Dough," as in lots of money.) "I live right over there." She motioned up and over the stand of trees out by the garages with her free right arm. "My husband, Ralph, said he wasn't interested in coming with me tonight but wait 'til I tell him about that young woman, Karumba. Her stuff is every bit as exciting as . . ."

At this point, evidently realizing she still held my limb in a viselike grip, her zeal suddenly replaced by embarrassment, she dropped her hand from my arm and her gaze to the ground. But after collecting her emotions for a few moments, she looked earnestly into my eyes and continued in a much quieter voice. "What I mean is . . . I just know he would enjoy the show as much as I have."

Well, there you go. Beauty was in the eye of the beholder.

Maybe, in this case, the beholder just had to be a little older. And that was OK with me.

"I'm pleased to meet you," I said sincerely. "My name's Scott and I've just now started . . . sizing up the pieces on my first pass through." I regretted instantly my ill-chosen verb.

"Oh . . . ?" She reached out and grabbed my right elbow once more, "Then you haven't seen Miss Karumba's work," her entire demeanor reassuming its former fervor.

Here we go again.

"You simply must see it. It's . . . it's . . ."

At that exact instant, out of the corner of my left eye, I spied someone whom I never would have imagined I would be relieved at seeing . . .

"Fabian," I hailed heartily.

Fabian Mortenson had not seen me until I called to him and when he did, I perceived what appeared to be, momentarily at least, a wince on his part.

"Scu . . . uh, Scott," he responded, recovering immediately upon spotting Virginia Mathews. "What a pleasant surprise," beaming in her direction. "Colleen mentioned today," he continued, "that we just missed running into each other at her place . . . in Malibu." The "in Malibu" appendage having been added for the sake of impressing my moneyed and eccentrically dressed acquaintance, no doubt.

Mortenson always did have an uncanny and unerring nose for wealth, or at least for those people who were willing to spend enough money to convince others of it. And now he was eagerly looking back and forth between my new "friend" and me, waiting expectantly for me to make good on what I "owed" him for not simply spitting in my face upon seeing me.

Under the circumstances, I jumped at the opportunity.

"Why of course, Colleen's place . . . in Malibu."

I figured if it was worth flaunting once, it was worth flogging twice.

"Well, you know me," I continued, "busy, busy, busy. In fact I saw Dale Childs today about his entertainment unit. Seems there was some mix-up about the TV." I smiled cheerily. "But that's all taken care of now."

Now, that was a wince.

"But enough shop talk," I said. Turning toward my newfound companion, I motioned in Mort's direction, "Mrs. Mathews, this is a friend and business associate of mine," laying it on "Dagwood-style," as Fabian likes it—really thick.

"Fabian Mortenson, ASID." The professional acronym "cherry on top" applied to the introduction like a rubber stamp to a bill . . .

PAID IN FULL.

Then, looking at Fabian who was now simply glowing, I said, "Fabian, this is Virginia Mathews . . . of Beverly Park."

Chaaa-ching.

At this point, at least as far as Mort and Virginia were now concerned, I no longer existed. And that was fine by me.

My ice had melted, I was sick of looking at Pole's pole and I needed to hit the bathroom. Exit, stage left.

Chapter Nineteen

It's an unfortunate fact of life that if you're going to consume liquids at a party, you're going to sooner or later have to use the bathroom.

That's not a particularly big deal if you're at a friend's house, or even at a small gathering hosted by someone you just met, because unless you party in the Ozarks, you'll most likely be able to use an indoor bathroom.

However, in a situation like tonight's "little get-together," where there were quite possibly three hundred people in attendance, it meant one and only one thing: "portable facilities." And indeed, as I was informed and directed by liveried help, that was the case.

Fortunately for me on two counts, I only had to go "number one" and, being a guy, I could take care of that standing up.

However, as I made my way down a lighted garden path toward the "bathroom," I was suddenly struck with an eerie case of *déjà vu*.

The stand of trees I mentioned earlier, now looming directly overhead in front of me, seemed strangely familiar.

In fact the slope of the walkway I was proceeding down and the entire bowllike topography of the surrounding space, seemed to contest my sense of "here and now" with another somewhat unsettling sense of "here and then."

I stopped in my tracks to take stock of my feelings.

I wasn't drunk. In fact, the surge of adrenaline that had started to course through my system had quickly ruled out the possibility of even being high.

No, as I scanned the tall, indistinct and now somewhat foreboding shapes of the dark trees and shrubbery that stood mutely around me on three sides, my senses keened with alertness.

It wasn't, however, until I turned fully around—facing back toward where I had just come from—and saw the massive three-story façade of the main residence, that I knew what was happening.

This was the house I had briefly worked on four years ago. The one that had that mammoth master closet Nacho and I had furnished the custom milling for.

Sure, at the time, the huge driveway had been just dirt, and there hadn't been any lawn, trees or shrubs around the main building, but the stand of trees behind me now, had been there, as had all the shrubs on this side of the property—probably planted by the adjacent neighbor. Of course.

Virginia Mathew's house had been farther along than this one had been at the time. And in an attempt to ensure that they had a modicum of privacy and quiet after they moved in—but while this property was still being worked on—the Mathews had trucked in and planted all this dense vegetation.

Now, I remembered.

And by another extremely odd coincidence, the "porto-potties" available to the construction crew back then had been located in just about the same location as the ones being used for this party now. That's why the things in this corner of the property had looked so familiar to me.

This was the house with the master closet. Wild.

Having sorted this out, I felt immediately calmer. But before turning back around and resuming my pilgrimage to the "john," I made a mental note to try and get another look at that closet tonight before I left, if I could.

It had really been something.

Once I had concluded my business down the hill and had rejoined the throngs of partygoers milling around the great front lawn, I "put up my antenna" in an attempt to pick Marney out of the crowd.

When I was a kid, this antenna technique, first introduced to me by my mother, had invariably worked when she would ask me to help her find a parking space in an otherwise crowded market lot. Since then, I'd continued to employ it with great success, clear up to the present.

And sure enough, there she was. And God, so were Bernard Weston and Horatio Blaire, both decked out in red leather jumpsuits, black fedoras and spats. Creepy.

As I finally approached Marney and the two men, I could hear Weston gushing, "And being a successful artist can open up a lot of doors to the interior design side of things."

"Hi, honey," I said as I joined them, giving Marney a proprietary peck on the cheek and nodding to Bernie and Blaire.

"Scott," Marney said with a relieved smile. "I was hoping you'd catch up with me. I've just been talking with Bernard and Horatio here about my work. It looks like they might have room for someone like me in their stable of artists. Isn't that exciting?" She looked at me expectantly, now.

I tried to rationalize away the watermelon-sized lump of dread that suddenly materialized in my chest upon hearing Marney's words. I really did. But in the end I couldn't, so, instead, I just lied.

"That's cool," I said, forcing the words out with a big "smile."

However, when I turned my gaze toward the two men to spread a little false cheer in their direction, my "Wow, that's really keen" machine died and all I could croak was, "That's really goo . . . uh, nice." Which withered as soon as it crossed my lips—a real conversation stopper.

To cover up, I went into a "swallowed something down the wrong pipe" act, coughed a few times for added effect, and hoped everyone, including Marney, would buy it.

Bernard signed off on it in a fidgety, relieved manner. Marney said, "Are you OK, Scott?" and reached over to pat me on the back, but Blaire just looked at me with dead eyes—like Lee van Cleef in the movie *The Good, the Bad and the Ugly.* Double creepy.

Then as if playing back a prerecorded message, Horatio announced in my direction, "You know, Scott, it's very rare that an artist comes along with the exact vision and voice to speak to an entire generation. But Bernard and I are betting that Marney here . . . ," switching his gaze back to her and nodding, "given the proper guidance, of course . . . ," his smile looking more like a grimace, "could be one of a handful of artists that can. In fact, we want to pursue that distinct and probable possibility," winding up his pitch with me back in his sights.

Triple creepy. I shivered to myself.

Distinct and probable possibility? That sounded more like high-flying bullshit to me than a "big break" scenario for Marney.

I mean, the stuff she'd told me about the night before sounded good, really good, but vision and voice of a generation? *That's laying it on a bit thick,* I thought.

And how did Pole fit into this? Certainly his work couldn't possibly be considered on a par with Horatio's plans for his artists to "speak to an entire generation."

Or was it? I guessed it would depend on what Pole's real "work" was, and which generation Horatio was talking about—remembering the lather Virginia Mathews had been in when I first met her.

However, when I looked back over at Marney, her blonde hair framing her smiling face like some radiant halo, I knew that I was going to have to keep quiet about my misgivings. At least for now.

But there had to be a way for me to get her away from these two flimflammers without stomping on her dreams in the process. Only, how?

Hmmm . . . A real brain teaser.

"Ah, Pole, here you are," Weston exclaimed, pulling my attention away from my own thoughts and onto the handsome man who was approaching us.

My God.

In person, Pole was one sexually charismatic man—a hunka, hunka burning love in a white silk shirt, tight jeans and black Italian loafers. His jeans were so tight in fact—"lizard-proof" as my mom used to call the style—I could tell from ten feet away that should a member of The Cumbers ever fall sickly and unable to cut their "harmony parts," Pole would be able to "fill in" nicely. No problem.

But just as Weston launched into introductions, my attention was drawn to a delicate arc of pearlescent droplets on the collar of Pole's shirt, just below his neck.

I was deep in thought, contemplating this oddity, when a voice, "'Ello, mate," brought my mind back to the present and I suddenly registered four pairs of eyes on me, one set belonging to Pole who was also extending his hand to me.

"Pleased to make your acquaintance, I'm sure," he said warmly.

His British accent and his easy smile threw me for a second but I managed to take his hand and shake it anyway.

In person, it was plain to see why people—both women and men—were attracted to him. He was a juicy piece of steak or a hot fudge sundae, or whatever else one might want to take a big bite out of.

And his portraits, no matter how much they were selling for, didn't do him justice. Did I mention he was handsome?

Anyway, at this point Marney, Bernard and Horatio moved off to the side and resumed the somewhat hushed conversation that they had been having when I first came up, leaving Pole and me more or less to ourselves.

It was Pole who spoke first.

"Bernie and 'Ornblower . . . ," nodding over toward Blaire, "tell me Marney might be joining our little gallery of rogues." This little witticism, in his opinion evidently, warranted a sly wink and a smile in my direction.

"Well, things are a bit preliminary, but that's what they're talking about," I responded tentatively, still trying to determine the "lay" of the land, so to speak.

"You her manager, then?" smiling first at me and then leering at Marney, the word "manager" sounding more like "pimp" the way he said it.

"Just a friend," I said, stealing a sideways glance at Marney to see if she was registering any of this. However, she was listening and giggling to something that Blairc was whispering in her ear.

"That's good. Friends are a nice thing to be able to fall back on in this business," he said cryptically.

"And what business is that?" I countered, finally getting tired of being on the receiving end of so much innuendo.

Pole took a second or so to assess me and finally said, "You've seen my work. I'm no Ansel Adams."

More like Grizzly *Adams,* I thought. *Or maybe* Gristly *Adams. Oh, what a wit I am.*

"All's I can say is, ever since I connected up with them two blokes . . . ," he hooked a thumb in their direction, "my work's been selling like bloody 'otcakes and I'm driving a Jag, 'stead of a Ford Escort."

Pole eyed me some more and then continued. "What business am I in? You seem like a smart lad. You figure it out. And if you and your friend still want to get in on some of the action . . . ," Pole once again leered in Marney's direction, "you'll probably do all right, yourselves."

So there it was.

Although I had thought it might be something like this when I first saw Karizma's handbill for tonight's reception, it still felt like a big empty hole that I was falling into.

With that, Pole said, "Good luck, mate," and turned to rejoin Bernard and Horatio.

"Oh Pole . . . ," I thought I'd take a chance. "You missed some," I said, looking at him in what I hoped was a meaningful way.

At first his expression was blank, but then he reflexively extracted a handkerchief from his shirt pocket and reached toward his mouth.

"No, the shirt. Just there." I nodded to the droplets below his chin.

"Oh," he said, tucking his chin into his neck for a look of his own. "Overspray," he smiled crookedly as he wiped the substance from his shirt. "I missed it. Occupational hazard these days. Man o' the house here wanted a little 'input from the artist' on the 'meaning' of the piece Horatio just sold him for his library—twenty-five thousand dollars, it was. Wouldn't take Karizma for an answer, so I obliged him myself."

"Shit happens," I responded ineptly, feeling very giddy in a surreal sort of way.

"That too." He grimaced and held my eyes in his for a second or so. "But what the hell. There's no such thing as a free lunch, is there?" Pole apparently was mentally assessing his own situation now. "Life's a bitch, ain't he?" With that, a weary aura settled over him, and he turned and walked off to rejoin the others.

God damn it, Marney, I thought as I watched him go. *What are you about to get yourself into?*

But instead of grabbing her—running screaming to her car and getting the *hell* out of there—I turned and walked, as if in a trance, toward the main house, without saying anything else to anybody.

Of all the derivations I've looked up over the years, the one for "cynic"—Greek *kynikos*, 'doglike'—is one of the more interesting I've studied.

But sometimes, even when it's justified in being suspicious, a constantly barking dog can be very annoying. Especially when nobody wants to hear it.

Woof, woof.

Chapter Twenty

Building a custom home can be one of the most enjoyable activities one can be involved in and yet, at the same time, one of the most demanding; remodeling an existing one, even more so.

The process is aggravated in part due to the fact that most homeowners—who are used to buying their food off the shelves at the market, their clothes off the rack at the mall, and their car off the lot at the dealer—can find the complexities inherent with a custom experience fairly overwhelming.

Consequently, when something "goes wrong" from time to time—and how could it not when you're building something out of thousands of individual pieces, by hand?—the client can start to worry that it's somehow "the contractor's fault."

However, in addition to the complexities involved with construction in general, I believe there's another (and even more unfortunate) factor that can work against builders: namely, the prejudice held by some homeowners that contractors are basically guys who, by some dubious natural *de*selection process, fell undersized through openings of opportunity that would have otherwise led to loftier careers—like golf balls through an automated egg sizing machine would do—and by default wound up working in construction.

And this bothers me. Why? Because, as I mentioned earlier, I admire people who are creative and build things.

I digressed into this topic because as soon as I entered the main house, I was struck once again with how great it is to help create something as satisfying as a beautiful home. Even though I had entered the building from a side door, far less grand than through the main entrance, the room I found myself in was still magnificent in its own right.

I let my eyes caress the elegant detailing evident even in this comparatively modest part of the house. Subtle mouldings unobtrusively ringed the junctions where the ceiling met the walls and the walls met the floor – a rich oxblood terra cotta. The walls themselves were finished in a subtle, straw-colored plaster effect, reminiscent of the work I'd seen in pictures of Italian villas.

The lighting from above, completely adequate as far as the illumination of the room was concerned, was again understated in terms of where it was coming from or, indeed, where the fixtures themselves were located. The effect, even now at night, was both sunny and warm. Masterful.

And then it struck me, what I was doing, without even having been consciously aware of it. I was on my way to see the beautiful master closet that I had helped create.

It's a funny thing, but even after a project is complete and the "rightful owner" has moved into occupancy, to a certain degree the work always belongs to the people who built it. It was with this conviction as fortitude—in case I ran into anyone who might contest my presence—that I mounted the back stairs heading for the third-floor master suite.

It took me a few minutes to get my bearings, because spaces that had once been dominated by scaffolding towering to the twelve-foot ceilings now contained ornate and beautiful furnishings—mirrors, armoires and tapestries gracing the walls, while hardwood, stone and carpeting alternated underfoot from room to room.

When at last I got closer to where I thought the master bedroom and closets were, I found myself navigating more by a sense of sound than of sight. For what had at first attracted my attention as a soft, singsong mewing, like that of a small animal, had increased in volume and intensity to the point where my curiosity was piqued, and I found myself homing in on it, master suite or not.

As I came around the last corner and the walls fell back to form the sweeping expanse of the master bedroom that I now remembered, I realized that the sound, a low keening moan at this point, was indeed coming from the walk-in closet, just through the set of huge double-doors to my right.

I was softly padding across the thick bedroom carpet heading in that direction, half enraptured, half scared shitless, when I heard a young woman's voice.

"Now you're getting it. Umm hmm, just there." And then the fevered moaning again, like some small animal in pain.

I stopped dead quiet and listened.

"Yeah, yeah, oh yeah." The woman's voice ebbed and flowed with intensity. "You've really got me going, girl."

Girl?

"Now take me up and over the top. That's it . . . gently. Oh . . . ooh . . . *oooh,*" the mewing escalating all the while.

There have been a few times in my life when an irrepressible, willful curiosity—an undeniable urge to see, do or feel something—has gripped me, and I've done things that were, strictly speaking, against my own "better judgment": such as the first time I got laid, the first time I took LSD (regrettably), and the first time I took off on a ten-foot wave.

And now it was happening again. But this time, as a *voyeur*.

Swell. Yet, I still couldn't rein myself in.

So I peeked around the door leading into the closet as tentatively as a man could do who was being held back by nine horses but driven forward by ten.

And stopped short.

For looking directly into my eyes with the flattest expression that I'd ever seen of anyone in her "position," was Karizma, reclining buck naked on an expansive leopard-skin chaise with what appeared to be the head of a woman in her lap.

Hello.

And then Karizma's voice started up again.

"That's it girl, do me," her eyes registering nothing but nothing. "Take me over . . . up and over, way up . . . way, way up and over," sounding as if she were pleading, but with still nothing in her eyes. "That's it . . . yes . . . yes . . . *yes.*"

And then suddenly, convulsively, she arched up, shaking and trembling in the process . . . holding it . . . holding it . . . holding it . . . until there was nothing left except her eyes, as flat and dead as ever, chilling me with their cold embrace.

At this point the "animal" sound that I'd heard outside started rising too, up . . . up . . . up in volume. Lapping and mewing greedily. More and more and more, and then . . . then a moan began, like the death rattle of some poor creature, letting all the life it had left in its body out in a rush.

"Oh . . . ooh . . . oooh . . . *oooh.*"

Finally the woman rolled away from Karizma, down onto the plush carpet, and just lay still for what seemed like a full minute, the sound of heavy breathing being her only outward sign of life.

And during this entire time, Karizma defiantly maintained her same repose—her taut stomach muscles and lungs working from her recent exertion—holding my gaze in hers, still completely expressionless.

Suddenly, the spell was broken and I returned "to reality."

What the hell am I doing here? I thought to myself.

But just then the figure of the older woman—fully naked herself, with her back still to me—struggled to her feet and, once upright, leaned over Karizma and gave her a small peck on the cheek.

"Thank you, dear, that was wonderful. Don't bother waiting for me. I'm going to take a nice, long Jacuzzi bath and we'll talk tomorrow about the placement of your painting in the living room." With that, she headed off to the bathroom through a door in the far wall of the cavernous closet.

As for me, one half of my mind was screaming, *Get out of here,* while the other half was refusing to obey. Back and forth, back and forth my conscience raged, like a soul-wrenching tug-of-war.

But after less than a minute—like I knew I inevitably would—I found myself standing inside the closet looking down at Karizma, who was still lying back, tauntingly, upon the chaise lounge.

I'm not certain, but I think she may have expected me to collapse into a little boy's "I tink I saw a pooty tat," or some such reaction, and to have run away by then. But I hadn't. Nor could I have accommodated, even if I had wanted to.

For I was struck stone solid from my head to the ground—a boulder of jammed incoming thoughts, recollections and "what might have beens"—at the sight of her naked yet still strangely allureless body.

"Feona . . . I . . ." The words hung acrid-sweet in the air like pot smoke at a rock concert.

But no further words came to me, nor even individual thoughts. For they were all still too compacted to allow one strand of sense to be separated out from all the others.

So I waited and watched—in the way that a mindless bug on the wall might have done—until, at last, Feona/Karisma climbed to her feet in wooden resignation.

"It's been a while, eh, Scuz?"

She spoke calmly, apathetically, her back to me now as she pulled on her jeans and buttoned the fly.

It was then that I noticed, completely apropos of nothing I could fathom, that the cowboy shirt she next pulled on over her breasts was red plaid with a decoratively stitched yoke, similar to the one that Virginia Mathews had been wearing. I guessed the cowgirl look was coming back in.

"How the hell you been?" Feona sat down on a small sofa to pull on her cowboy boots (no socks), her voice still void of any apparent emotion.

"I don't know. . . Good . . . I guess," I responded dully, still feeling really wacked.

"*Good, I guess* . . . would be . . . *good* . . . I guess . . . huh?" She eyed me appraisingly, for the first time.

After what seemed like hours of silence on my part, I finally grabbed one thought, one emotion from my otherwise still logjammed head and heart and blurted out, "What the hell happened, Feona?

"I mean . . . hell. What happened?" I gamely but lamely repeated.

Feona took her time responding to me, sweeping up her hip shitkicker cowboy hat from a nearby table instead, placing it on her head, then languidly posing and adjusting it in front of a full-length mirror.

When she was finally satisfied with her look, she turned toward me, assuming a slouchy stance reminiscent of a high-class fashion ad, and said, "Who's asking, my older sister's ex or the guy I gave up my cherry to when I was seventeen?"

And that, thank God, cleaved the boulder in my head and heart in two. One half for the distant past—as Feona's lover, the other for the recent—as Shelly's ex. And I could at last feel all my thoughts and emotions start to unpack.

But still I pondered her question for a long moment. *Which way should I go?*

Until, finally, I decided to throw my lot in with the recent past. Hoping to somehow bring the distant one of Feona and me up into some kind of reconciliation with it in the process.

"I'm . . . sorry Feona . . . I . . . Shelly's ex," I said, finally just letting the words fall where they might and hoping that she would still stay on the line, still want to talk.

But if she did, it was going to be her decision. Because I'd done everything I could do to span the gulf between us. So I waited once again.

I could see her thinking about it, estimating the advantages and disadvantages to keeping the channel of communication open between us. The wrongs that had been done: first by me, and then, in seeking retribution, by her. And then the time: the time back then; the time that had gone by 'til now; and, finally, if she decided she wanted to have it, the time we might still share in the future, as friends.

I guess in my mind it was even money, either way. But in the end, thankfully, the future won out.

And as that old "water under the bridge" cliché goes, the belligerence that had kept her body taut, though previously invisible, ran out of her like an electrical charge going to ground. Then her face softened into a wry smile, and she said, "Ah, hell, Scuzman, I hope you got better with Shell because you sure were one sorrowful piece of ass with me."

With that, I crossed the few feet left between us, took her in my arms and held her gently until she'd stopped crying.

Then we got the hell out of there.

Chapter Twenty-One

It felt good to get outside again, out into the open evening where things didn't feel quite so heavy with the deadness that had come over me upstairs.

I was methodically working the cool night air into and out of my lungs, over and over again until I must have started hyperventilating, because it was just at the point that a couple of million of my brain cells were effervescing and exploding like bubbles in a glass of seltzer water, that I caught the sound of Smitty calling my name.

Fizzle, pop, p-p-pop pop, fizzle, ". . . uzman. Man, are you deaf or what?"

And then casting a quick glance over my right shoulder toward Feona, he called out, "Oh, hi Marney. I've been trying to find—" the fact that Feona wasn't Marney suddenly registering on him.

Guys can get kind of tongue tied in the presence of a beautiful woman in general anyway, but especially when they've mistakenly "overreached" and made a connection of familiarity with one whom they are, in fact, unfamiliar—as was the case now with Steve.

"Uh . . . you . . . uh . . . I . . . uh . . . uh . . . ," said Steve, looking back and forth between Feona and me, not knowing which of us to address or, indeed, what he should say once he'd decided.

This went on for a few long seconds until Feona, out of either sympathy or irritation, I don't know which, finally put him out of his misery.

"Howdy," she said, bending forward and extending her right hand like a politician "pressing flesh" in a crowd, but eager to get it done with and back into the limo.

However, when she made contact with Smitty's hand, he grabbed hold of her like one of those woven Mexican novelties that you can't pull your fingers out of once you slide them inside. And he just wouldn't, or more likely couldn't, be shaken off. Because, Feona was trying.

Feona, at last sensing Smitty's momentary lapse in mental capacity, stepped out from behind me and let her still-captive arm go slack, a benign smile settling on her face like a celebrity who has realized that she's just going to have to ride out the next few seconds, until her star-struck fan regains enough motor control to release his grip.

Which Smitty finally did.

But Steve, who had (absolutely) been drinking, followed the handshake up by gushing shamelessly, "God, I'm so horny for you."

Without missing a beat, Feona replied, "Well, needy guys aren't really my thing." Flexing the circulation back into her hand, "But thanks anyway. I'll keep that in mind."

"With that touching exchange out of the way," I said, looking first at Steve, "Smitty," gesturing toward Feona, "this is Karizma." Then, looking at Feona, "Karizma," motioning back at Smitty, "this is Steve Smith—faithful sidekick, cabinet finisher extraordinaire, demented artist."

"Demented artist, huh?" said Feona, registering a genuine interest in Smitty for the first time. "What do you know. Now that, I can go for from time to time." And she extended her hand to him again, but meaning it this time.

"The pleasure is all mine," said Smitty, finally responding appropriately and taking care not to crush her offering this time. "I assure you." A real Don Juan.

"By the way, lover boy," I asked Steve, "you seen Marney?"

"Who? Oh . . . Marney. Last I saw her was forty-five minutes ago, over there." He motioned with his head, still goofily fawning over Feona. "With Horatio, Weston and Pole."

"Swell," I muttered and turned to survey the dwindling throng of revelers down on the great lawn.

Looking . . . looking . . . *bingo.*

There Horatio was, standing out in the crowd like a red leather fireplug.

It's interesting how a person can become aware of the attention that another person is extending them from a distance—like they're being bombarded by a wave of fine particles (which maybe they are). At any rate, Horatio looked in my direction the instant that I spotted him, and he immediately started moving toward us.

When he was within earshot of us, he extolled, "Karizma, my star," and beamed at her. "Dorothy tells me she simply loves your piece."

Boy, he could say that again.

"I see you and Scott have already met," he remarked, shifting his gaze to me. "That's great." And now back to her. "Scott's girlfriend, Marney, is thinking about joining our little family."

Now it was Feona's turn to blanch.

"I didn't know you two were . . . together," she said, looking at me questioningly. "She's . . . uh . . . a really good artist . . . a good person." She cast a nervous glance back in Horatio's direction.

"Yeah, well . . . ," I said, just letting it drop, never taking my eyes off Blaire.

"Say, Scott," said Horatio, being the first to resume speaking. "I've got the keys to Marney's VW. She wanted me to give them to you."

"Her keys?"

"Yeah. She said she was feeling a little too tipsy to drive. Bernard volunteered to take her home."

What is he talking about? I wondered. *Marney doesn't get "tipsy."*

I was still trying to figure that out when Blaire continued.

"Besides, there were some pieces that Marney expressed an interest in seeing at the gallery. Since it's the same direction as her place, Bernard and she decided to stop by there on their way. Figured it would save her a trip tomorrow. Said you wouldn't mind." Looking at me steadily now, the ball in my court.

I didn't like it, but I figured Weston was harmless enough. Besides, what was done was done.

But I did decide to do something else.

"Say," I said to Horatio, guiding him out of earshot by his arm—which I noticed, somewhat to my alarm, was thick, muscular and hard. "I don't know what you and Marney talked about in terms of her working with you, but . . . ," I swallowed and steeled myself to say it, "I think you better forget it. It's not going to happen."

Blaire, extricating himself easily from my grip, squared around to face me, adopted an amused look and said, "Oh?"

I decided to press forward.

"It's a cozy little thing you and Weston have got going here." I let the words hang with as much meaning and menace as I could muster. "But Marney's not your girl. She's not for sale."

"Not for sale?" He feigned incredulity. "That's the goal of all artists: to have their work presented and sold to an adoring audience. I mean, take Karizma," Blaire went on, persisting in the charade. "She was selling her paintings out of a garage when I discovered her. Now look at her."

"Yeah, they're really lapping her up."

Now that one landed, I could tell.

The only trouble was that instead of becoming embarrassed or flustered at being caught in a lie, the pupils of Blaire's eyes merely dilated, not out of apprehension or fear, but as if he were a predator, a T-Rex perhaps, registering only the "what," "where" and "when" of the encounter.

Not good. And then he spoke.

"I don't know what you're getting at, *Scuzman*," he sneered, moving into my space for intimidation value now. "Bernard and I run a reputable business and any public insinuation on your part to the contrary will be of extreme interest to our lawyer, I'm sure."

He was glaring at me now, but I learned a long time ago how to deal with assholes like this. Especially when the odds are somewhat even.

I mean, what was the worst he could do, hit me? Not likely, with so many people around.

"Look, you maggot . . ." I wasn't as big and fit as he was, but I could still do some damage. "You go near Marney again and I'll break your fucking arms."

Stupid and laughable as my "threat" was—the likelihood of me being able to break one of his arms in a fight would be slim, but to break both of them, damn near impossible—he nevertheless stopped advancing, which was good enough for me.

However, in the body language of hate that is as old as mankind, he "said," *I'm going to get you.*

And with that, he turned and walked off down the lawn toward the tented gallery.

Oh, joy.

"Hey Scott," Smitty said, ambling up to me from where he and Feona had been talking. "Karizma and I want to go see Stand Tough play tonight at this club on Pico. You want to go?"

"No," I sighed tiredly. "I've had enough confrontation for one night."

"Well, what I mean is . . . Karizma's ride, you know that rapper that was performing earlier? He left."

With that, Steve fell silent like a child might when presenting a parent with a problem - the implicit communication being that if the "grownup" doesn't do something to solve it, things will somehow get even worse.

Great. I fingered Marney's keys in my pocket, while the inevitability of going clubbing with these two night owls settled over me.

I guessed that meant Feona would be spending the night with me on my boat, which was fine by me. I definitely wasn't going to let her go home with Smitty, at least not on their "first date."

That would give Feona and me a chance to talk. Maybe I could even help her.

Ah hell, I thought, looking at Smitty who was now doing that "pity me" thing with his eyebrows that can be so annoying.

"All right, let's go," I said and trudged off toward the car, the two "lovebirds" in tow.

At least I was going to get to test drive Marney's beetle. That was something good that had come out of the evening.

Chapter Twenty-Two

The drive down from Mulholland by way of Laurel Canyon and then on south of Sunset to where it becomes Crescent Heights was uneventful.

And I must say, Marney's Beetle handled every bit as well as I had hoped it would.

Furthermore, the only time when I felt like a sissy was when I handed the keys over to the valet in front of the club on Pico.

The car was yellow after all. I simply know he thought I was gay, the savage.

Stand Tough N B Counted hailed from the south Orange County area around Laguna Beach—"The OC" as it's now known. Though extremely popular and well attended down there, the band had made a trip north tonight in hopes of broadening their fan base to include Los Angeles County—or I guess, as one might say if they were as silly and cynical as I, "The AC."

Come to think of it, if things went well in The AC, they could try to crack "The VC" (Ventura County), head back south to "The DC" (San Diego County) and finally breeze back into The OC, full-fledged southern California celebrities.

Yeah.

However, judging from the marquee outside the club announcing "Stand Tough N B Mounted," one would think the band still had a ways to go in terms of getting the word out.

In spite of this promotional glitch, Stand Tough turned out to be a group of truly fine songwriters and musicians. So good, in fact, that I could feel the stirrings of "what might have been" that I sometimes get with regard to my own past musical aspirations.

You see, when I was in my early teens, I wanted to be a musician and write songs. Or at least, that's what I thought at the time. For it eventually turned out to be more a case of "earnest self-delusion" than anything else.

I remember it well . . .

It was after seeing one of those old *Million Dollar Movies* that they used to broadcast on Friday nights—one starring Dean Martin in a corny Tin Pan Alley songwriter comedy—that I "decided" writing songs was indeed my "life's calling".

My only problem—or, let me rephrase that, first and foremost problem—as I pursued this ambition was that my "muse" was imitation and my artistic voice was mute due to the fact that I had nothing, really, of my own to say to anyone.

In fact, as I look back on it, my entire "plan" to become a successful writer of popular songs seemed to be based on emulating the lifestyle depicted by Martin in that movie. Namely, a songwriter didn't have to communicate with anyone except an amusing sidekick of his choosing (for comic relief), gorgeous women (plenty), and a mildly irascible yet very supportive agent who dropped by the writer's "party pad" from time to time to deliver rave reviews as outlined in the morning paper, and royalty checks—lots of royalty checks.

Additionally I extrapolated—and this was the real clincher for me—if Dean could manage to not talk with anybody he wanted to, get laid and collect lots of money in New York, well then he could probably do the same thing in San Francisco, Paris or wherever.

Needless to say, with this as a career "foundation," my efforts over the next few years were met with very little success in terms of getting my music out and recorded by others.

But, in a weird way, this was actually a good thing. Because when I finally did decide to call it quits, I wound up reconnecting with something that I had more or less taken for granted and dismissed prior to this: designing and making cabinets, something that I really was good at (even on a bad day,) and about which I did have something to say artistically.

And so it was as I let Stand Tough's ode to entry-level movie work, *Piss Ant,* wash over me in joyous contentment, that I realized I was finally at peace—like a snake might feel having shed a dead skin—with not being a musician anymore.

And that alone was worth having stayed up late for.

"Hey, Scuz," Smitty leaned over between songs. "You know there was something I wanted to talk with you about, something about Blaire and Weston."

"Oh?"

“I can’t help feeling I’ve run into those guys before.”

“Yeah, where?”

“That’s just it, I can’t put my finger on it.”

I fell silent, thinking it might help him think, but Smitty just slumped back down in his seat, took a swig of his imported beer and put his attention back on the band.

Thanks, Mister International Man of Mystery.

And the band rocked on.

Chapter Twenty-Three

Later when the three of us had started back for the Marina—me driving, of course, Feona riding "shotgun" and Smitty in the back seat, asleep—Feona turned and eyed me tentatively.

"You know, I don't want you to start getting all worried about what . . . what happened tonight."

I was glad she had broached the subject because I hadn't even known where to begin. And since she'd started it, I figured I'd best say as little as possible.

"How's that?"

"I know how it looks."

That made two of us.

"But, I've got it under control." She looked to see if I would contest that, but when she saw that I didn't, she continued.

"You've got to understand something about me that maybe you never . . . hell, maybe I never knew about myself until . . . until just recently. I mean you . . . you always had working with your hands and Shell . . . shit . . . Shell always had you. And then when you two didn't work out and you moved to L.A. and she . . . she set her sights on the high life, well . . . I kind of just felt like I was the one left out . . . with nothing to show for myself." She was looking down now, wringing her hands in her lap.

"I know I'm going around in a big circle on this, but the thing is . . . the last few years, for the first time in my life, I learned I was somebody . . . somebody with something . . . something big inside to say."

She wasn't looking at me now but straight ahead, straight out the windshield, and it looked like she might be wiping her eyes, but in the darkness I couldn't tell.

"You see, after you two were gone and I'd finally gotten out of high school . . . ," the last two words spoken as if she spat them out, "and I started hitting a stride at Orange Coast College, hitting my stride with my art, well, I finally felt like maybe I could have something special too." She looked across at me in the darkness to see if I was still listening, and I was.

"And it got better and better and the ideas and the work started to flow, and for the first time in my shitty life, I felt like I had really tapped into . . . into something special . . . into me . . . *into me,* you hear?" Her voice was rising now and I could see Smith in the mirror, stirring from his stupor.

"Hear what?" Steve was still drowsy and trying to make sense of the voice he was hearing, but we didn't pay him any attention and he dropped back off.

"By the time I had finished school I was starting to sell a few pieces. Not anything big, but I was starting to get some things in galleries around Laguna and I was starting to become known . . . starting to finally be able to pay for my art supplies, for Christ's sake. And as the years passed, it kept getting better. I eventually moved into a little place in Laguna Canyon, a garage really, and I was making the rent and I was building a following, and I was . . . you know, making it, making it with my art. And then I won that contest." And with that her voice cracked and she did break down.

The sobs started coming from deep inside her, and I started having more attention on her than on my driving and that's when I almost clipped some doofus in the middle of the street on one of those three-wheeled, "I'm reclining in a seat while riding a tricycle" contraptions.

Stupid idiot.

Fortunately, by now we were on Admiralty Way in the marina and I only had a couple of blocks to go to my boat. So I put my attention back on the road, eased my grip on the wheel and listened for Feona to come out of her crying jag.

As I pulled into the lot adjacent to my boat, she stopped.

"Yeah. That damn contest," she hissed angrily. "I wish I'd never entered."

"I entered a contest once," Smith volunteered cheerily from the back.

"Shut up," I howled over the seat at him, and immediately felt guilty for doing it.

"I'm sorry . . . Smi . . . Feona . . . continue."

And she did.

"They hold a contest in the summer around the time that all the 'sawdust' stuff is going on."

For the reader's information, the city of Laguna Beach has long cultivated the atmosphere and identity of "an artist's colony," which undoubtedly it once was. But with the passage of time and the escalation of real-estate prices, this quaint and picturesque image has required more and more "cultivation" to maintain—"working-class artists" probably stopped being able to afford houses there in the mid-fifties, if they could have afforded them even then.

So as part of the effort to keep the tradition going, and as a nice thing in its own right (I'm not completely cynical), the "Festival of the Arts" has been a big deal there every summer for decades.

But, of course, as "culture" tends to do, the festival got richer and stuffier the more time that passed and more attention was paid to it. Until, sometime back in the sixties, I believe, in somewhat of a hippy "counterculture" rebellion, I would imagine, someone came up with the idea for more of a "back to basics" art festival to be held across the street from the "big one."

They called it The Sawdust Festival, for the folksy atmosphere and the wood shavings that were scattered around on the ground of the various outdoor art viewing venues. And that's what Feona was referring to by "sawdust stuff."

With that bit of historical background in place, let's allow Feona to continue.

"Anyway, I was at home in my studio one morning, trying to take advantage of the glorious summer light that used to stream inside at about nine o'clock." Feona seemed to smile at the recollection.

"And I get this call. *You've won.* And I can remember thinking, *Won?* like it was maybe some condo promotion or something. So I hung up." And at the thought of this, Feona allowed herself another smile.

"So the phone starts ringing again and I pick it up and before the lady on the other end can say anything, I say, *You're wasting my light,* and I hang up again," the smile on her face starting to fade.

Then, turning wistful, she said, "And if I only had left it at that . . . instead of finally answering when she called the third time, well . . ." And then she started to cry again but this time like a soft brook that was in no hurry, the tears just coming at their own pace.

After I waited in silence for what I thought was a respectful period of time, I asked, "And then what happened?"

"It's funny you should ask that. Or should I say, it's funny you should ask that after I've asked myself that same question a million times? The weird thing is . . . ," Feona looking at me now, "I don't know."

And then continuing, "How did I go from creating my art, having a great life and feeling really happy to . . . to . . . what happened next? I mean I can't even figure it out looking back at it." She shrugged hopelessly.

"Well, what did happen?"

"Well . . . I won the contest. And then they held an award presentation for me. I was all dressed up in my newest-looking pair of old jeans. I mean it never even occurred to me that my picture might wind up in the paper." She laughed weakly.

"I guess I felt a little like someone who had stumbled out of a time capsule and suddenly found herself newsworthy. Pretty soon I started getting glad-handed from every quarter. Gallery owners who hadn't given me the time of day ever started calling me at all hours. New artist 'friends' I didn't know, and whose work I'd never even seen, started hanging around my studio. I mean it was just a garage and it got to the point where I needed to hire someone to pick up all the empty Starbucks cups that people were leaving behind. It was a zoo."

Pausing as if to rest, Feona let out a long, tired-sounding sigh and then at last continued, "So about a month of this went by and I started getting less and less work done and feeling more and more displaced in my own home, where just weeks before I'd felt the happiest I'd ever been in my life. And then, of course, to 'ease the pain' as they say, I started drinking heavier than I was used to. Needless to say, that didn't help, so, genius that I am, I started smoking pot . . . which, believe it or not . . . ," suddenly looking at me, "I never did as a kid when you knew me. *Honest.*"

She looked like she might need a response from me, so I said as gently as I could, "I believe you, honey."

Satisfied, she continued, "But then, when that didn't work, well . . . ," she let out an even bigger sigh, "I did the only thing that a girl in my situation could do. I started snorting coke. Naturally." Sarcastic now, "Why not? It seemed like a good idea at the time." Then, resting her head in her hands, she said, "God, what a mess."

At that point she fell completely silent for what seemed like a couple of minutes, save for the sound of her breathing. As for me during this time, I tried to completely disappear, as if maybe any sound, or movement or anything I did would yank her attention crashing back to the present from what she was looking at. And there was no way I was going to do that. This was her life and whether she told me about it now or ever, it was going to be her decision to continue to talk about it or not.

So I waited. And after what seemed like the longest single moment of my life, she picked up again.

"But here I was, a newly minted minor celebrity, and everywhere I turned there was someone who was more than happy to give me something to get high on. It was depressing, really depressing," her voice barely a whisper now.

"So, eventually, I wound up pretty much doing anything and everything—sex too." She looked at me forlornly, "Everything except creating my art," shaking her head as if to say *NO* to herself. "Then after a spell of that, I started looking for a way out."

Feona looked at me searchingly now. "You know what I mean by 'out', Scott?"

I thought about her question for a bit and then said, "Yes, I do," remembering the time right after Shelly and I had split.

Feona appraised me with a sidelong glance for a few long moments and when she was evidently satisfied, she said, "Yeah, I believe you do," smiling weakly. Then she picked up her own story again. "So anyway, a few weeks ago when everything had gotten about as low as it could go, well, I met Weston and Blaire at a party." She sighed and stared bleakly into space, no doubt running the pictures in her mind.

At first I thought she was going to run from what she saw but when she sagged in the seat like death warmed over, I knew that she wasn't. She was going to ride it all the way down. And I was going to let her do it.

"I feel so degraded," she finally said in a voice just louder than a whisper. "So damn degraded." And the tears started to flow again. "Before I even knew what I was starting to suspect, man, it was game over. I couldn't have gotten away if I'd wanted to. They had pictures," she choked out between sobs. "Dirty, filthy pictures of me." And then she really started to bawl.

"I mean, do you really think I'm so messed up that I could actually let some rich old broad go down on me and think, *Hey, no problem . . . just as long as the check clears*." A wildly agitated expression was now in her eyes.

"Tell me, Scuzman, do you think I'm that messed up?" But then without waiting for a reply, she blurted, "Because I sure do. And that's what's been killing me."

Then she broke completely down and cried and cried and cried.

And I let her because it was like letting the poison out. The poison that had been eroding her dignity and killing her spirit for the last several weeks was finally being released. And so she cried and cried and cried some more, and even Smitty, who was wide awake now, didn't say a thing. Which was good, because if he had, I would have strangled him with his own seatbelt.

Afterwards, when she was all cried out, Feona turned to me and said, "Scott?"

"Um?"

"Will you help me?" she asked, little worry lines forming on her forehead, but her manner now much calmer.

"How so?"

"Uh . . . I know you know. That is . . . what I'm trying to say is tonight . . . that wasn't the only time I've done . . . I've done things for Weston and Blaire that I . . . don't feel good about. And, I was wondering. That is, I think . . . if I don't tell someone else about them . . . tell another human being about them . . . like right now, tonight . . . well, I may never do. And if I never do . . . I . . . I don't know . . . I just feel like I may never walk in the sun again. If, you know what I mean. So if . . ." But she just let the rest go unspoken, waiting for my reply.

"Smitty, you can crash on the port settee, if you want." And I tossed him the keys to my boat. "Feona and I are going to grab some coffee and talk for a while."

And we did—or, more correctly, she talked and I listened—about artists and art, blackmailers and fame, money and admiration, happiness and sex. And in and amongst all that, Feona talked about the things she had done that had brought her to the brink of giving up on herself.

Until somewhere in the night, she came back to herself. And forgave it all away.

Now that was one of the best conversations I've ever had. And I never said a single word.

Saturday

Chapter Twenty-Four

It was still dark outside when the ring of my cell phone brought me partway out of a dream having something to do with Jell-O and a baseball bat.

"Scuz." It was Ron Kimmel again, the guy I'm supposed to be trailer-sitting for.

"Don't hang up," Ron said.

I let that pass.

". . . annel 5 . . . now . . . Haven't . . . to . . . stayed . . . Mojo Mill . . . Tuesday . . . I'm coming home." And then his line went dead.

I must have been getting used to Ron's superabbreviated style of communication, because I simply switched on the little TV I keep on my boat and tuned it to channel 5.

No doubt it was going to be another one of his cryptic travel updates.

At first the screen remained silent and black, but then over a thrumming chorus of nylon-stringed guitars, a man's voice jubilantly announced, "Buenos días, LOWS HANG-AY-LEEZ. Eeees time for the *Chi Chi Argentine*

Ess-shooowww. L.A.'s numero uno drive-time news program."

Suddenly, out of the darkness, like a multicolored phoenix rising from the ashes of night, sprang a hot little number dressed in full flamenco regalia. With her feet pumping like a pair of small pistons and her trim body arched back provocatively like a diminutive bullfighter, her arms and hands flowed gracefully over her head, intertwining in a seductive pattern.

"*Buenos días, muchachos y muchachas,*" she hailed in a throaty voice. "The time has come to wake up, smell the little beans of coffee, and *vamonos al trabajo.*"

With this she let out a series of shrill yelps and proceeded to undulate around the studio floor to the now trumpet-laden music.

Holy shit, I wondered in amazement to myself, *What the hell time was it anyway?*

The bedside clock responded in mute illumination: 5:00 A.M.

Just then the music broke and the screen went to a commercial.

"Friends, are you tired of . . . ," a voice started droning as I swung my feet off the starboard settee, where I had sacked out across from Smitty, and walked, still sleep-ravaged, the three feet to my boat's tiny bathroom.

By the time I got back, Chi Chi had evidently changed, for she was now sitting behind her news desk, professionally attired in a "power suit," the style favored by female lawyers.

"Annie Hurricane. What is it that I can say? She is one angry *pendejo*. Let's go to Buffy Martinez in south Florida, to check her *out.*"

With that, the camera cut to an attractive Latina whose blonde bouffant hairdo was being buffeted about by the wind like a bulbous jellyfish in a riptide.

"*Chi Chi,*" the young newsperson wailed into her mike over the roar of the wind. "It's hot and sticky, and having to hike out here onto the beach like this . . . well, it reminded me of that Ricky Martin video I did when I was first getting started in the business." Buffy laughed at her own attempt to establish a lighter tone in the face of the otherwise "dark and dire" circumstances she found herself reporting on. "But enough about me. The real story is that shack down on the edge of the sand dune over there."

With that, the camera panned across the beach to where a hammock, once stretched between two palm trees, had fallen to the sand in front of what appeared to be a small fishing cottage.

"Until yesterday this was the home of long-time resident Mojo Miller." Martinez paused for dramatic effect. "But sometime late last night, Mr. Miller may have become Hurricane Annie's first victim.

"For, you see, according to some," she eyed the camera ominously, "Mr. Miller is believed to have been swept out to sea when he tried to retrieve the beer he had tied to a rope out in the water. Still others, who wish to remain anonymous, told us Mojo was so despondent about losing his job on the recently ill-fated *Polly Want a Pirate Too* shoot that he may have decided to take a one-way midnight swim. And though both these reports are just titillating speculation, we thought you ought to be aware of them.

"Unfortunately in the presence of an inconvenient lack of hard evidence," she continued with a smirk, "the local authorities are being stodgily hesitant to attribute Mr. Miller's mysterious absence to Hurricane Annie or anything else of possible interest to our viewers. Therefore in order to keep a flow of provocative information coming your way, we thought we'd do a little investigative reporting to kick things up a notch."

With that Buffy winked impishly into the camera, said, "Follow me," and resolutely walked over and opened the door to Mojo's tiny abode.

It wasn't clear what happened next, but what appeared to be the bare ass of somebody lying in a bed just inside the doorway at first filled the screen and then, just as quickly, was replaced by a view of the ceiling of the room.

Just then, a man's angry voice could be heard ranting in the background, and what seemed to be the loud report of a gun flat-lined the audio feed.

What followed next was the chaotic view from a camera, evidently being carried on the back of someone running away down the beach: palm trees . . . sand . . . feet . . . sky . . . Buffy with a terrified expression on her face . . . more trees . . . more sand . . .

At this point the audio feed came back on line, ". . . upid bitch and *stay* out," but stopped as quickly as it had restarted, for apparently Buffy, who had been looking backwards while running with her microphone in her hand, ran right into a palm tree.

And then the feed cut unceremoniously back to Chi Chi in L.A.

"*Dios mío, Buffy,*" exclaimed Chi Chi in mock concern, watching her own monitor. "Watch your head, girlfriend," playfully perky again, "your next perm is on me."

"Good Lord," I groaned.

Was it me or was the whole world going insane?

I flicked off the set and went back to sleep.

Chapter Twenty-Five

About 10:00 A.M., Feona, Smitty and I went out to breakfast. Though obviously tired, Feona looked ten years younger than she had the night before.

After we'd ordered our food and Smitty had gone off to forage for some sugar, Feona reached across and put her hand on mine.

"I want to, you know . . . say thanks for last night."

"Ain't nothing but a thang, baby," I cracked, for whatever reason deflecting the appreciation that was both heartfelt on her end and deserved on mine.

What was that all about? I wondered.

"Scu-uz," she said, withdrawing her hand in mild protest, "I'm serious." But still smiling. "No kidding. You really listened, you know, and it helped."

Maybe that was it. Maybe I just wasn't used to "being there" for someone else. I guess I'd fallen out of the practice without noticing it, after Shelly and I had split.

"'Course, I'm still up to here with Fred," she continued, lifting her hand to her throat. "He's still got the pictures and all, but I've got myself back and that's the best it's been for quite a while." Breaking into a really warm smile, she went on, "So thanks again, even if you don't believe me." And she blew me an air kiss.

"No, no, I'm sorry. I do believe you. I'm glad I was there, glad I could help." Looking back into her eyes, "It was good for me too," I said. And I reached over and patted her hand in return, as Smitty slid back into his end of the banquette. "But, Fred?" I asked. "Who's Fred?"

"You know," she said, seeming a bit surprised by the question. "The hicks." But when she saw I still didn't understand, she added, "The guys I told you about last night: Bernie Weston and Fred Blaire. The hicks . . . from Fresno?"

"That's it," Smitty suddenly exclaimed, nearly spewing his coffee across the table. "Fred Blaire, Fresno State. I knew I'd seen him before."

"What are you guys talking about?" I asked, looking first at Feona and then at Smitty. "Who's Fred Blaire?"

And then the penny, nickel, dime, et al., finally dropped.

Fred Blaire, a.k.a. Horatio Blaire.

"Oh my God," I gasped and my head started to swim with the ramifications. "Wait a minute," I finally managed, looking at Smitty. "You're saying, you knew Horatio . . . er . . . Fred at Fresno State?"

"I didn't know him, but I knew who he was. He was in a livestock class I was taking."

"A livestock class? Horatio Blaire?"

"Yeah, I was still up in the air about my major and—"

"Forget about that, Smitty. I mean I'm not trying to be rude, but it's just . . . Let me just get this straight.

You're talking about Fred Blaire, the guy I almost got into a fight with last night. The gallery owner. West Side dandy. Bernard Weston's partner. That Fred Blaire? You're positive?"

"One and the same."

Smitty was beaming now, obviously enjoying being "the man in the know."

"He was majoring in animal husbandry when I was there. I guess that didn't work out for him," Smitty added, pensively.

Didn't work out? I thought. *Au contraire.*

I'd say that Fred had made more of his college major than most.

Who said the modern college system was doomed to failure?

"Oh and now that I think of it . . . ," Smitty piped back up, "I remember Bernie too. Fred and he used to hang out together. Bernie was a drama major."

Again I marveled at the postcollege continuity. Those two boys had really gotten their money's worth from good ol' Fresno State.

"Bernie used to rehearse his lines for the plays he was in, out by the corrals."

"Corrals?"

"Yeah. I thought it was strange at the time, but I figured it was like working in front of an audience—the cattle and all. Actually," Smitty yelped, apparently remembering something else, "Blaire used to practice his routines there as well."

"Routines?"

"For the cheerleading squad. He used to really freak out those cows, let me tell you. You know, *GOOOOOO*

BULLDOGS. That was Fresno State's mascot," he added. "Billy Bulldog."

(Note to reader: If this is incorrect and yet somehow still got by my publisher's fact checker, please, for the sake of poetic license and the "bigger picture," just let it slide. I promise I will not persist in hoodwinking the American reading public regarding this point should it ever be legitimately contested during an interview with a nationally known talk show host. Thank you. The Author)

"You've got to be kidding." Now it was Feona's turn. "I was joking about Fred and Bernie being hicks," she said, looking first at me and then at Smitty. "I just overheard Fred saying to Bernie once, *Things could be worse, we could be back in Fresno*, or something like that, and from then on I always associated them with being from the sticks. That's wild."

For a few seconds, the three of us stared at one another in utter amazement, not saying a word, just mentally watching all the dominoes drop, fanning off in all directions. But then one particular run caught my attention.

"Oh, shit."

"What?" Feona and Smith asked in unison.

"I'm thinking about Marney," I said, fixing Feona with a fearful stare. "Last night you said something like, *Before I even knew it, it was game over. They had pictures*. What happened, exactly?"

"Well, like I said," she began slowly, "they slipped me a Mickey the first night I came up to L.A. I didn't even know it had happened until—" And then her face turned white. "Oh my God, Scott."

My thought exactly, but I had already started jabbing Marney's number into my cell.

"What are you guys talking about?" Smitty asked. "And while you're at it . . . ," he went on, looking at me but nodding to Feona, "how come you keep calling Karizma, Feona?"

I eye-motioned for Feona to fill him in while I impatiently waited for Marney to pick up.

"Come on, come on," I urged. "Oh, thank God," I said, when I heard her voice, but then, "Shit," realizing it was just a recording. "Marney," I blurted, once her greeting had run its course, "it's Scott. Call me as soon as you get this. It's important. Don't talk to anybody, especially . . ." But I decided not to go there, on the phone. "Just call me first. OK?" And I hung up.

Feona must have given Smitty the *Reader's Digest* version of her life because by the time I'd hung up, she was telling him about the gallery scam.

"Man, that really sucks," Smitty pronounced once he'd gotten the gist of what she was saying.

"Yeah," Feona continued. "I wouldn't be surprised if Bernie slipped her something last night so that she couldn't drive home."

And then seeing me grimace at that, she said, "I'm sorry, Scott. Really, I am."

But I was already back deep in thought.

"They couldn't get pictures that fast, could they?" I finally asked, looking searchingly into Feona's eyes. "I mean, bad ones. Horatio stayed at the party and I can't see Bernard—" Feeling too depressed at the thought, I dropped it.

"No, Scott," Feona said, trying to reassure me. "I don't think we have to worry about that. With someone like Marney, even some nude stuff would probably be enough." Then, noticing my newfound assurance slipping away again, she added, "But that's good news. What I mean is that the pictures probably wouldn't have to be that bad for her to feel really embarrassed—for her to feel like she had to do whatever they told her to do."

She was right, of course. But it wasn't just the pictures I was worried about. It was what would surely follow.

"Now if they do have pictures," Feona continued, "and I'm sure that's what Fred's intentions were last night, she's in a tight spot, what with the gallery's grand opening tomorrow night."

"Opening?" I asked. "I thought—"

"That was just the preview," Feona corrected me. "Didn't Fred tell you?" But then, judging by my expression, guessing he did not, "With the renovation of the gallery finally complete, they're having a grand opening to celebrate it. It's supposed to be a big deal." Turning to include Smitty now too, she went on, "All their heavy-hitter clients will be there—TV, the major L.A. art critics, maybe a thousand people or more. Jeremy and I were scheduled to attend but since Fred saw me with you last night, I'm sure he knows I'm not going to make it. That's why he's really pushing on Marney to take my place."

"Who's Jeremy?" It was Smitty asking.

"Oh, Catchpole. Jeremy Catchpole, the other artist there last night," Feona replied.

"You mean Pole?" I asked, making the connection.

"Yeah," said Feona, laughing. "Pole. God, that's a stupid name."

Again for a few long seconds, the three of us sat silently contemplating the situation.

"Speaking of Po . . . uh, Jeremy . . . ," I looked at Feona, "what does he think about Bernie and Fred? I mean if push came to shove, do you think he'd help us with Marney?"

"Absolutely," Feona replied, without having to give it a thought. "He's got nothing to lose. The money's been good for him, no doubt," she admitted, "but he can't stand either of them. And you know, after last night," she continued, "you can count on me, whatever you need."

"That goes for me too," Smitty announced gallantly. "Those two A-holes have got to go down."

Well, that made four of us: Feona, Smitty, Pole and me.

But we were going to need more help than that to pull things off—that and a plan, of course.

So, like a kid sleepwalking in a dark room who's gradually waking up to the fact that he'd better start figuring out where all the furniture is, I began thinking of ways we might extricate Marney from her situation. A situation that, unfortunately, she was absolutely convinced was the greatest thing since run-flat tires.

When at last I came across an idea that I thought might serve, I asked, "How would you guys like to go to a party?"

"Party?" Smitty asked, brightening up at the prospect.

"Yeah," I answered. And proceeded to outline the devious little plan that had started to form in my mind involving crashing Horatio's opening.

Chapter Twenty-Six

"Yo, Dawg." It was a skinny white kid dressed in butt-crack jeans riding down past his boxers, an oversized black T-shirt with the words *What you say?* on the front of it, gigantic unlaced sneakers and a Yankees cap with the bill facing at a dutifully oblique angle. He was standing in the parking lot above my boat, his voice blanketing the entire general area as if directed to everyone and no one at the same time.

A black mountain of a kid dressed all in purple—sneakers, jogging suit and silken do-rag—was motionlessly occupying nearly two cubic yards of space right next to him, humming.

Feona, Smitty and I had come back to my boat after breakfast, with Smitty immediately retrieving his skateboard and heading off toward his place to look for something I had asked him to find. Feona had mentioned that she'd arranged for the rapper at last night's party, "Maize N J," to swing by and pick her up sometime this morning, so while she was below deck freshening up, I had gone topside to keep an eye out for him.

And now it appeared that he had arrived, "with posse." Their black tricked-out Hummer and purple Escalade were parked behind them in the lot above.

Before I proceed with this humble narrative, I would like to take a minute or two to touch on an interesting male phenomenon that has in relatively recent years been elevated to a near art form by young western males in general, and coincidentally, Maize N J here in particular.

This phenomenon primarily concerns the public preoccupation of some men with their "privates," to use a euphemism my father's mother liked to use. Although there are many varied manifestations and mannerisms connected with this phenomenon, the central activity boils down to something that could be termed "checkin'."

Checkin' is in essence the action of a guy grabbing his crotch in full view of everyone else around him. Although this moronic territorial gesture seems to be the humanoid equivalent of a dog pissing on a fire hydrant, it is never performed simply as such. On the contrary, this declaration is always conveyed in a roundabout manner as if the guy doing it has some other legitimate reason for "checking" himself in public.

These "reasons" (among countless others) include such self-aggrandizing pretenses as:

A) Checking that his "member" is getting proper and adequate ventilation (because of the heat generated by its enormous size);

B) Checking that his (immense) "package" is not being chafed by the close proximity of the clothing shrouding it; or

C) Checking that the required blood flow to and from his huge "wang" is not being impaired because of (again) its inordinate dimensions and the constricting western cultural convention of having to wear pants, as opposed to, say, a kilt, loincloth or nothing at all.

Whatever the pretended reason is, however, the actual message imparted by checking oneself is always some variation of, *I'm large and in charge,* or *You want some of this? You can't handle this.*

Additionally, whether for style, obfuscation, or both, the genital grab is usually performed as part of a choreographed dance with other "cock of the walk" struts and gestures. And at this moment, Maize N J was "doing the dance."

Shoulder roll, foot drag, slide step, *checkin'.*

"Yo." The pimply-faced little geek fixed me with a theatrical glare. "Lookin' for K-girl. You be knowin' where she be?"

Struck dumb, I was.

Neck roll, eyes shut, reverse roll, eyes open, shoulder bob, *checkin'.*

"Axed me to come by and picks her up."

Checkin'.

Was this moron for real? Words just would not come.

And now, evidently taking my muteness for some form of defiance in response to his question, he lit into an orangutan arm swing, double foot shuffle, head weave, *checkin'.*

And then again, *checkin'.*

"Yeah, white boy, talkin' to you." The words were directed at me, but then he did a droopy-eyed head roll and body arc back toward his one-man posse . . .

Checkin'.

"Yo, Heavy M," addressing his companion now.

Cross-armed hand dangle, *checkin'*.

"I'm gettin' more attitude from this guy than I wanna deal wit."

Arm fling, head dip, finger splay, grimace, *checkin'*.

"Whyn't you go down and read him the four-one-one."

Hair groom, double shuffle, side slip, shadow box, *checkin'*.

And now the glare at me again, *checkin'*.

With that, the big black kid opened the gate (without apparently needing to unlock it first) and started ambling down the ramp toward where I had stepped out onto the dock to meet him.

Not good.

Meanwhile, up on the sidewalk, the dance continued.

Big smile, pretty boy, wrist wobble, half strut, *checkin'*.

When the mountain finally spoke, it was with a softness that surprised me. "Monroe Washington's the name." His smile hidden from Maize N J, above, he said, "Don't mind him, he's an idiot," extending both fists to me, which I butted with mine.

Hand drape, hip swivel, knuckle crack, *checkin'*.

"Wants to be a brother so bad it not only hurts him but everyone around him. He went to Beverly Hills High, what can I say?"

"Good to meet you, Monroe." I kept my game face on for Maize N's sake, "Scott Kuzman. Call me Scuzman."

Butterfly side step, torso twist, shake it off, *checkin'*.

"What's your tie-in with the wigger?" I nodded toward the upper walkway.

Arm fling, matador, toreador, back door (I'd never seen that one), *checkin'*.

"We're on the same record label. I go by Heavy Mettle, with two *t*'s."

I couldn't suppress the smile. "Mettle?"

"Yeah, it's a hoot, huh? Most kids don't even get it, but I keep trying to put a positive message out there with my lyrics anyway. The literacy level in this country really sucks."

"Yo, Dawg." Again from above.

Chest puffed, head faint, shake it off, shoulder roll, *checkin'*.

"Ho be there o not?"

Fade left, slide-step, grimace, arm fling, *checkin'*.

"Dumb ass," Monroe muttered under his breath and shook his immense head. "Right up," his voice boomed up to where Maize N J had apparently gone into a variation of The Bangles' "Walk Like an Egyptian," then, *checkin'*.

"The guy doesn't even know his name means *corn cob up my ass*, if you think about it." Monroe smiled tiredly. "His daddy's a big trial lawyer in town—Nathaniel Jessup. That's how he got signed. Rapper boy is NJ the Third."

Checkin'.

"Ahh, street life," I said.

"Yeah, it can be tough."

Half spin, double-handed hair groom, flamenco heels, *checkin'*.

"Say, if there's any way you could take Feona . . . er, Karizma . . . instead of Maize N . . . ," I asked the big man, letting the reasons go unspoken.

Spin, spin, spin, *checkin'*.

"Not to worry," the understanding clearly in his eyes. "Feona and I go way back. I been away at Harvard the last four years but I knew her before then."

"Harvard?" I blurted.

"Yeah, business law, top ten in my class," the pride evident now in his demeanor. "Fell into rapping on a fluke but it took off, so I went with it. Feona and I knew each other when I lived in Newport Beach."

"Newport?"

I was beginning to feel like an incredulity dispenser.

"Yeah, that didn't make my artist bio either," Monroe smiled wryly. "I was born in the Bronx. My dad was a plumber. When I was eight he invented the Hush-a-Flush and sold it to the highest bidder. He couldn't stand the winters so we moved out to So Cal. Been living on Lido Island ever since. It's very white, but very nice. Known Feona since just after you married her sister."

"No shit." I was flabbergasted.

"Feona and you are both good people." He smiled warmly. "I'll watch out for her like family."

Half nelson, full nelson, Ricky Nelson, *checkin'*.

And with that, I took Monroe down into my boat to get Feona.

By the time Monroe, Feona and I were back out on the dock about twenty minutes later, we had expanded upon and refined my initial plan for crashing the gallery opening. Monroe had even come up with how we could enlist Maize N J and a full posse from the record company to fatten up our ranks.

I liked it.

Fortunately, a bevy of female Japanese tourists had deluged Maize N J for autographs while we were below, working things out. That had kept him pumped up and feeling good about himself, which was nice, considering the alternative.

Things were definitely starting to shift in our favor, or so I thought.

Chapter Twenty-Seven

"You have three new messages," my phone informed me. "First message received at ten-seventeen A.M. . . ."

"Hey Scuz, it's Karl. Your truck's ready. Five hundred dollars cash, or six hundred dollars check. Take your pick. I'm here until noon."

Click.

"Second message received at ten-forty-seven A.M. . . . ," my phone droned.

"Thanks for the knife in the back, Scuzman." (It was Marney.) "You know how much this gallery opportunity means to me and for you to try and sabotage it is just . . . just . . . really a betrayal. (sobbing) Go to Hell."

Click.

So much for recruiting Marney to help bring down Horatio.

Oh well, Colleen would help me talk some sense into her.

"Third message received at ten-fifty A.M. . . ."

"You louse."

Not good.

It was Colleen.

"How could you say those horrible things about Weegee?"

What the hell was she talking about?

"I'll never ever put him on antidepressants and for you to even suggest that is . . . is . . . sickening."

What?

"And don't bother calling about my office project either. Bernard says he can find someone else who can do it."

Click.

Shit, I thought, *Horatio*.

I should have seen this coming. Now what was I going to do?

I was still trying to figure that out as I drove my revitalized pickup truck north up along PCH toward Paradise Cove.

Though the sun shone golden on the water, happy beachgoers flocked and frolicked all along the way and the fresh smell of the ocean wafted through my cab, I just felt numb. Stupid, inadequate and numb.

When I finally pulled up in front of Ron's trailer, the first thing I noticed was my job portfolio lying in a disheveled heap on his front door mat.

Walking up to it, I saw a piece of paper clipped to the cover.

It had a one-word message scrawled on it . . .

Don't.

Well I guess that said it all. God, I felt lousy.

That's when my legs turned to Jell-O and I "sat" (dropped) down on my ass like a fighter going down for the count.

When I finally snapped out of it, things hadn't changed for the better.

What a surprise.

The situation reminded me of one of those TV ads: *Do you feel unhappy? Hungry? Tired? Short? Fat? Broke? Well, if so, you need to start self-medicating.*

I only wished it were that simple.

I really did, but alas . . .

So I decided to go for a walk to clear my mind.

I hadn't gone fifty yards before some of the dots started to connect up and hold hands. There were only four main players in this little nightmare I was in—Horatio, Marney, Colleen and myself. The only trouble was, it was three against one and Horatio wasn't exactly "playing fair."

Again, no surprise.

But there was still one person Blaire probably hadn't been able to directly block me on: Weegee. And judging by the way the two of them had hit it off at Colleen's yesterday, it wasn't likely that Horatio would try to go there himself. He'd rely on Colleen to do it for him.

Ergo, Weegee was where I was going to have to start turning things around. There, and maybe Fabian Mortenson.

Mort was a long shot for sure, but I couldn't afford to dismiss him as a resource at this point. He'd be another way I might be able to reach Colleen.

The good news was that Horatio probably wasn't even aware that Mortenson and I knew each other or that Mort was in the running to design Colleen's job. I found myself hoping that the little social favor I'd done Mort last night—introducing him to Virginia Mathews—would still hold value today.

Finally, looking at the ocean for the first time since arriving back at Paradise Cove, I noticed that the south swell from yesterday was still running. It was then that I had a stronger than strong hunch that one of the tiny surfer dots I could see way up the bay at Little Dume was Weegee. So I headed in that direction.

As I left the perimeter of the park behind and trudged out onto the sand north toward the point, I started to relax and I could feel a modicum of life—hope, really—starting to seep back into my step. I don't know whether it was my newly regained sense of purpose at speaking with Weegee, the focus that physical exertion can conjure up (brisk walks in soft sand are hard work), the amazing beauty of the cove (as always), or all three, that accounted for my lift in spirits, but, whatever the reason, I was thankful for it.

I had walked about half a mile when I did indeed spot Weegee dropping into a silken six-footer. The wind had dropped to zero and the surface of the wave looked like oil. It was going to be a good ride.

Even though it wasn't me on the wave, I couldn't help but project myself into Weegee's place: the surge of exhilaration as you become one with the forward rush of water at first take-off; the joyous equilibrium of forces at work as you drop down the steepening face of the swell and then carve deeply into your turn; the hiss and wetness of the water all around you like water-skiing as your board starts to plane and pick up speed; and the roar of the wave like a friendly lion that's come out to play with you again. Back and forth, back and forth, the give and take of the water and sun and the feelings and sounds of being at one with such a beautiful force of nature—a cresting wave. Not life-threatening but definitely powerful—maybe even more than a thousand horses. But circularly, like life, 'round and 'round, spiraling forward, racing toward its own climactic apex and then, once reached, spiraling still, but ever more and more gently back down to a oneness with the timeless ebb and flow of the ocean.

Man, that was a great ride, I thought.

Thanks, Weegee.

I'm not sure whether Weegee had seen me and wanted to talk or if it was just good timing on my part, but as I came up abreast of where he had just finished his ride, he started paddling toward shore.

The moments in life that I tend to dislike the most are the ones I spend in anxious anticipation. And this was one of them.

What, if anything, had Colleen said to him about me? Did he still consider us friends? I didn't know, but I was about to find out.

It was Weegee who spoke first.

"Surf's still . . . hot," he opened tentatively.

I was relieved that his usual rhyming banter was, at least for the time being, on hold.

"Yeah, that last wave was really something," I responded as I watched the last remaining drops of salt water run off the sleek mane of his long hair into a tiny rivulet all down along the side of his black wetsuit and finally across and over his bare foot to the sand.

"Say, Weeg," I began, "I don't exactly know where to start with this, but, something's come up and I really need to talk with you about it."

"Yeah?"

"I don't know if you heard but . . . all hell's broken loose between your mom, Marney and me."

I would have continued but I could see the beginnings of an amused smile taking over his face.

"What?" I asked.

"Oh nothing." The smile was getting even bigger but for some reason he was looking at his feet, trying to play it down.

"*What?*"

"Oh . . . I just thought it would be something like this," he said, shaking his head with an *I knew it* look on his face. "It's old Hornblower, isn't it?" he at last asked, looking at me now.

But when I didn't respond (because I'd rather have him tell me), he continued, "Yeah, well, I heard Mom talking with someone on the phone this morning. Must have been Blaire." He snorted. "That slug. He told Mom you said I needed to be sedated, needed to see a shrink." He was looking at me now like he knew I'd never say such a thing.

That was a relief.

"I knew it was bullshit, but Mom . . . she believed him and got really upset. He even started going on about how you thought Marney was a talentless wannabe. God, you should have heard the fireworks that went off when she called Marney about that."

Oh man, I could only imagine.

"I don't know what to tell you, Scuz," Weegee continued, looking at me sympathetically now. "You've got your work cut out for you with those two. They're really bent out of shape."

"Sounds like it."

It was a lot to take in but it was just as I had suspected, and now I could feel some of the tension connected with the dreaded mystery of it all starting to dissipate.

"I just had to see how you felt about all this," I said.

"That's cool," Weegee said, but then a look of puzzlement clouded his face. "How do guys like Horatio get away with stuff like this? He's obviously lying."

"It's just the nature of the beast," I said. And I did mean *animal.* "Guys like Horatio deal exclusively with making people feel worried or guilty, stressed out or upset, and some of it just sticks."

"You know, now that you mention it," Weegee hastened to add, suddenly looking a bit uneasy, "it wasn't just you Horatio was talking shit about. He started saying some stuff about me too. I couldn't really hear what it was, but afterwards, Mom started sort of grilling me about . . . you know . . . stuff." Suddenly he looked down and started to trace an imaginary circle in the sand with his big toe. "But there's no way that he could have . . . I mean . . . ," Weegee said, looking up at me pleadingly, but then, "Ah hell." And he dropped his gaze to the ground once again.

"Look, Weegee, this is what I'm talking about," I said, trying to will his attention back out from wherever it had gone. "Guys like Horatio punch around until they find something that you don't feel good about, are worried about. And then they jump on it and blow it *way* out of proportion. Then they'll work it and work it and work it until you just want to crawl under a rock and hide."

Weegee was still looking down, silently tracing the circle with his toe.

"Hey," I said, and waited for his eyes to come up and meet mine. "Don't worry about it, you're one of the good guys. We're going to blow him out of the water."

Weegee thought about that for a second or two and finally a somewhat relieved expression came over his face.

"Thanks, Scott." He smiled. "Count me in."

Chapter Twenty-Eight

I had called Mort and he had agreed to meet me at Innuendo on Santa Monica Boulevard for a late lunch. It wouldn't have been my first choice of a place to meet—or have even made my top 100—but I wasn't calling the shots at this point.

On my way over from Malibu back into West Hollywood, I reviewed my conversation with Weegee. I think the thing that struck me the most about him was how much more emotionally mature he seemed now than he had been the first time we met. And I couldn't help smiling at what I assumed he had been thinking about when we were talking about feeling guilty. God, that was a tough age.

On a more practical note, he had filled me in on everything he could think of that had gone down between Horatio, his mom and Marney over the last day and a half. Further, it seemed Weegee was very well connected with what could be called the "Malibu Mafia": a loose but fiercely supportive association of watermen and beach people—surfers, kayakers, sailors, fishermen; old, young, rich, and blue collar—all united in their love of and respect for the ocean. He had offered to show up at tomorrow night's opening with as many of his friends as he could. And since their ranks numbered in the hundreds, if only one out of ten showed up, it would be a huge help.

Yeah, *go Weegee.*

The allure of sex, it seems, is enhanced by the introduction of mystery, a glimpse of skin having much more attraction than "the full Monty" most times. This fact, I assumed, accounted in part for the selection of the name of the "bistro" Mort had proposed—for the place was little more than a meat rack with food a distant secondary concern, at least for the patrons. In short, Innuendo was the hot spot *au moment* in West Hollywood to greet and then hopefully meat (sorry) young and attractive men.

Now at this advanced stage in this book, I trust you're well enough acquainted with me to know that I'm not going to go off on some "gay-bashing" tack or take an overly "moral" tone about what happened at this meeting with Mort. But, I would like to comment on something that I have been absolutely dying to talk with somebody about for literally years.

What's the deal with the black leather motorcycle cap (*à la* Marlon Brando in *The Wild One*) that is usually so tiny and tight upon the head of the guy wearing it that it looks like a circus hat on a poodle? And the leather vest; tight little "muscle T" with some Lucky Strikes rolled up in one sleeve; leather chaps—bottomless, *naturellement*; and, of course, last but not least, a pair of Frankenstein-sized motorcycle boots?

Put them all together on a guy who weighs, say, 145 pounds max, plant a severely cropped little mustache on his upper lip, and you've got what?

What?

Please excuse me for being so obtuse, but is he the motorcycle or the rider?

Now esthetics, creativity, art, procreation and sex are all allied subjects, so I can understand how whimsical flights of fancy, in terms of fashion, can tie in to sexual attraction. But this particular mock-up—James Dean in drag—has always left me kind of feeling confused. Like how a gorilla might feel, trying to hump a medicine ball. You know, *Which end is up?*

But, enough of that.

As I entered the dimly lit interior of the restaurant and waited for the acute feeling of embarrassment to pass—born of the fact that I knew everybody present could see me, but I couldn't see a damn thing—I recognized the pulsing strains of "Born to be Wild" wafting through the air from some remote and discreetly located speaker system.

Oh great, they were playing my song.

When my vision finally adjusted to my new surroundings, I spotted Mort signaling to me from a corner booth and I couldn't help but feel for the second time in less than twenty-four hours how relieved and glad I was to see him.

We had to stop meeting like this.

"Scott." His smile was warm and his handshake seemed sincere. All I could think was that Mrs. Virginia Mathews of Beverly Park must have signed up for the full treatment. Why else was Mortenson being so cordial?

But as I sidled into my seat, I spotted the nearly empty highball glass to his right. He'd been hitting the sauce and fairly hard from what I could tell, because it was starting to hit back.

His forehead was moist with perspiration, face flushed and florid, and his eyes were aswim in their sockets.

My God, I thought, *tell me this isn't his second . . . third?*

I needed Mort to be able to remember this conversation the next day.

"Hi Mort," I said. And then as somewhat of an afterthought, "Good to see you."

"Good to see you too, Scott." He smiled.

It was?

"Sandy." Mort motioned to a diminutive waiter dressed like a little boy . . . a little French boy with a cute ass.

Cute ass? What am I thinking? I howled silently to myself. *Stop it, stop it, stop it.*

And without even registering what else Mort was saying, I blurted to no one in particular, "A beer. I need a beer. NO. Wait. Make that a gin and tonic—a double. Yeah, a double G and T, and make it hurt."

With that, I let my head fall into my arms on the table and waited for the shrill sound of the siren in my mind to recede.

It has been said that all men have a little of the feminine in their makeup and that women, some of the masculine. Well, I don't know about that, but since I am a wholehearted supporter of the notion that people are spiritual beings and not mere bodies—and in so being are actually themselves neither male nor female in nature (only their bodies are)—I believe that everyone has had a hell of a lot of experience on both ends of the "tennis court": good, bad and indifferent.

So, in light of this, I feel it's fitting—and I'm just speaking for myself here—that while I'm in a male body, I have sex with females and when I come back around as a female, well, then I take a run at the men.

But as I said, that's just me. You can take it or leave it.

". . . ott. . . Scott. Are you all right?"

It was Mort. He had his arm wrapped around my back and his face down close to mine.

"Unnhhh?" I managed.

"Jesus, Scott, I thought you had a heart attack." Then suddenly, "You didn't, did you?" a look of concern blanching his otherwise arterially reddened face.

Rearing my head back up off the table and regaining a bit of my naturally caustic self in the process, I responded, "No I didn't have a heart attack. It's just that . . . this . . ." Looking around the room in an irritated manner now, I ranted, "Why the hell did we have to meet here?" Leveling an accusatory gaze at Mort, I went on, "I feel like I'm at an orgy and everybody in the room's got a boner but me. It's sensory overload, man, I mean, what the hell. How can we talk business here?"

Then suddenly, as the heat of my exasperation started to dissipate, I saw Mort's face come into focus in front of mine.

That's when I felt bad. For before me sat a confused and upset little boy who had meant no harm. He had had no agenda but to meet me in a pleasant place (at least to him), share a meal and listen to what I had to say. It was me after all, who had asked for this meeting. And here I was, acting like a jerk.

At this realization, the music faded into the background of my consciousness and the needy horn-dog vibe of the room seemed to disappear. In fact, I could feel my whole center shift slightly and the threatening paralysis that had gripped me—that had felt so intense, so real just moments before—start to evaporate. And in its place I could sense myself settle into just "being there."

That felt good, and, what's more, it felt appropriate to the situation.

I wasn't cruising for a guy. I had Marney (I hoped).

So what was the big deal? Nothing.

"Uhhh . . . I think I got a bit overwhelmed there for a minute, Mort," I said, looking at him apologetically now. "Like I fell into a shark tank or something. It sort of shocked me, but I . . . I'm OK now. I apologize, I really mean it." And I did mean it.

Mort studied my face for a few seconds and then he broke into a relieved grin. "I know what you mean. This place can be kind of intense the first time." And then he turned and motioned to Sandy again.

By the time our salads arrived (real men eat salads too) I had decided against suggesting Mort switch over to Irish coffees, for it no longer looked like he was going to insist on drinking his entire meal.

He had ordered a Nicoise and I the Caesar, which was, to use a word I kept hearing in conversations at adjacent tables, *fabulouuus.*

For a while, we ate in silence and just enjoyed the fare, but when Mort cleared his throat and daintily wiped the nothingness that had accumulated on his lips while eating, I found myself a bit surprised, wondering what he was going to say. For I realized how mentally occupied I had been up until that exact moment, feverishly trying to conceive of and then mentally rejecting every conversational opener I could think of on how to broach the subject of the situation with Horatio.

"You know," Mort began. "It was a bit of a coincidence that you called about getting together, for I . . ." And he blushed? "I've been meaning to talk with you about something too . . . for a while."

At this point, Mort visibly mustered some resolve and looked me earnestly in the eye. What can I say? I was all ears except for the part of me that was spinning around like a mouse on a wheel wondering what he could possibly say next.

"I guess you could say . . ." He swallowed like he was fighting back the urge to keep on lying and instead was willing the truth to come out for once. "I've been being a bit of a fraud." Before I could figure out what he was referring to, he added, "What I mean is, living a lie."

Well, that didn't clarify things much but I didn't think any question I could ask would speed things up, so I just decided to let him get there on his own.

That's when the fidgeting started that sets in when someone is sitting on a real whopper. His variety was the finger bounce. *But what could it be?* I wondered, and I stopped eating my salad altogether.

At last he took the plunge.

"Look, everyone knows I diddled the invoices on the Petrie job." He looked at me forlornly. "I jacked that lady's budget to the moon and I admit it." He spat the last bit out. "But you have no idea how many times I've lain awake at night, wishing that I hadn't." A tear appeared now on his cheek and his breathing became labored like his lungs were filling up with tears too. Then he sobbed into his napkin, "I really have."

Whoa, I hadn't expected this.

After the tears were cried out somewhat, he continued.

"But, as they say, what's done is done—and I can't go back and undo it." But then he looked at me as if I might actually be able to offer him the answer he'd been hoping for. "Can I?"

I let some time go by to make sure he was really asking. And when he continued to look at me, I said, "No Mort, we can't go back. But . . . ," the hope in his eyes pouncing on this last word like a bum on a bologna sandwich, "we can do what's right. I mean, in the here and now." Looking at him with what I hoped wasn't a piously holier-than-thou expression, I declared, "It's never too late to take responsibility for something. If that's what you really want to do."

At that, he seemed to relax a bit, just a bit, but I could tell he was still sitting on something else. And then his whole body sagged and an extremely tired smile played across his face.

"The here and now. Boy, there's a concept for you." And he looked sideways at me. "You wanna hear about my here and now?"

His bleakness startled me and I blurted out the first thing that came to mind. "You don't have to do this, Mort . . . I mean . . ."

Oh hell, I thought, *just let him go.*

So I eased back in my chair and got ready for the ride down.

"Fabian Mortenson, ASID," he finally said, puffing out his chest in mock pride. "Sounds impressive, doesn't it?"

He didn't need any comment from me, so I didn't offer any.

"Well, let's work backwards, shall we?" he hissed through a cruel smile. "ASID . . . American Society of Interior Designers," he trumpeted grandly. "Phew, what a joke. I might as well append a couple of 'Ph.D.'s' while I'm at it," he said, and looked at me sourly. "Do you realize that in such a . . . a flimsy profession as this can be, where perception . . ." And with that he struck a scholarly pose—one hand grasping the lapel of his coat and the index finger of the other pointing heavenly. "Perception is KING," he intoned solemnly. "Or queen, as the case may be," he smirked. "Hell, I even faked that. I'm no more a member of that society than my mother is. And she's dead. I took a damn extension class on design from a study-by-mail place in San Diego and just added the *ASID* to my business cards, for Christ's sake."

Now I've seen guys get into moods like this where they seem to take exquisite pleasure in ripping themselves apart so as to "atone" for some (usually imagined or greatly exaggerated) shortcoming on their part. And it's not a pretty sight. But as much as I would have liked to stop him, I knew I couldn't, at least not now. So I let him roll.

"That takes care of my professional association." He smiled wickedly. "So what's next?" he continued. "Oh, of course . . . Mortenson. What's the deal with that?"

And he looked at me in mock inquiry. "How about *Jam*?" he asked, enunciating the last word in an ugly and unflattering way and then raising a graceful hand to his ear as if trying to make out a distant and delicate sound. "No, most decidedly not," he declared, assuming a look of theatrical disdain. "Well, guess what?" he asked, glaring at me. "That's my real name: Jam. Charming, isn't it?" Then, revving up like the product huckster on a TV game show, he warbled, "But that's not all. Tell them the real clincher, Morty." And he closed his eyes and seemed to start to weep.

After what seemed like a minute of nothing but a snuffling sound, he spoke in a whisper.

"Sam. Sam Jam. Pathetic, isn't it? I'm Sam Jam, the designer man."

And he sat silently for a while, no doubt thinking about what he had just said.

But after a minute or so he started up again, assuming a singsong tone.

"I'm Sam Jam, the designer man. Wham bam, thank you, ma'am. Sam Jam, the design—"

"Stop it, Mort," I barked and I grabbed his arm hard. "As popular as running yourself down and kicking your own ass until you bleed self-pity is nowadays, I have never, and I do mean *never*, seen it do a damn bit of good. You want to do it for a while? Fine. You want to throw yourself down the stairs? No problem, go ahead. But enough is *enough*. You don't have to make a career out of it."

"But, I—" he protested weakly.

"No buts," I cut him off. "We're not going to do this anymore. The game's over. The reason is, and here's the short version," I continued, "I need you standing and in one piece."

"What do you . . . mean?"

"You know the hassle that's been going on with Horatio?"

"I know about his shady gallery dealings," Mort said through a snuffle, "if that's what you mean."

"Well, there's that, but that's not all. Now he's going after Marney and me."

"Wh . . . why?"

"I told him I didn't want Marney involved in his scam and now he's trying to drive a wedge between her and me. He's crazy and that's the only word for him."

At this last assessment, I could see some skepticism creep into Mort's eyes.

"Look, you don't have to believe me," I said by way of sidestepping a debate. "It's just that I've had too much experience dealing with guys like him to kid myself otherwise. Just take my word for it, he's bad news."

Although Mort still didn't look entirely satisfied, he at last asked, "So what do you want me to do?"

"I just want you to be aware of what's going on and to be ready to maybe lend Marney and me a hand if it comes to that."

After saying this, I looked at him for any sign of support that he might be willing to pledge, but he just sort of looked drained.

"Besides," I continued, "I think Colleen could be next on his hit list."

Now that got him.

"Colleen?" he gasped, suddenly alarmed. "She's not in any danger, is she?" he asked, looking refreshingly concerned about someone other than himself for a change.

"No, not that I know of now. But she called and left me a message this morning—some nonsense about me wanting to put Weegee on psych drugs. Horatio was behind it. If she doesn't fall in line with his wishes, he may turn on her too. Just keep your eyes open."

"My God, that's so weird. She's actually the reason I wanted to meet with you today." This turn of the conversation seemed to revive Mort's interest in what he had been talking about before. "You've probably been wondering why I've suddenly developed such a case of scruples." He looked at me sheepishly.

"The thought did cross my mind."

"Well, it's just that she and I . . . you see . . . well, this gets into the other thing that's been part of my . . . my fraudulent life."

"Oh come on, Mort, you don't have to—"

"Yes, I do."

"Don't do this to yourself."

"God damn it, Scott, when I told you I was living a lie, I meant—"

"I thought we already—"

"*No.*"

"*Mort.*"

"*Please.*"

"*Stop.*"

"But you don't understand," he wailed. "*I'M . . . NOT . . . EVEN . . . GAY.*"

Seventy-five guys stopped talking at once.

Oops . . .

"Check, please."

Chapter Twenty-Nine

Before retrieving my truck from Innuendo's valet, who apparently considered pulling up in front of the tony little establishment in it so demeaning that he actually declined my tip, I had a few more minutes to talk with Mort about the situation with Horatio, in general, and what I was asking him to do regarding the gallery opening the following night, in particular.

To say that Mort's life had been "in flux" lately would be the mildest of understatements, and for that reason, I hadn't pushed things. He eventually promised to call me later and that was more than good enough for me.

After leaving West Hollywood, I decided against heading back to Malibu (and Marney) and instead drove toward my boat. Between last night with Feona and then talking with Monroe, Weegee and Mort today, I felt completely wrung out. Consequently, I was looking forward to getting an hour of shut-eye to re-charge my batteries before contemplating my next move.

However, halfway there, I got a call from Smitty.

"Where you been." More an accusation than a question.

"With Mortenson. Why?"

"Don't you answer your phone anymore?"

Smitty could be such a putz sometimes, but I swallowed my irritation and just said, "What's up?"

I could tell he would have liked to give me a little more shit, but the excitement that had prompted him to call in the first place finally won out.

"I found it," he said at last.

Smitty was referring to his copy of the Fresno State yearbook that I'd asked him to locate.

"Is it as good as—"

"Better," he crowed. "Better than anything we could have hoped for. And . . ." He let the word dangle. "We've got witnesses."

"What do you mean?"

"A couple of the girls on his old squad live in Venice. Can you believe that?"

I was drawing blanks for a second, until I twigged. "You mean, cheer-leading squad?"

"Correctamundo. Tracked them down on the Internet. They run a Pilates studio over on Rose Avenue."

"What did they say when you called them?"

"That's the best part." Again the pause for added effect. "They're willing to roast Horatio with a routine tomorrow night if we can get them some musicians."

I immediately thought of Heavy M and his contacts at the label.

"Tell 'em I'll get them whatever they need."

But even as the words came out of my mouth, it dawned on me how big this operation was becoming.

"On second thought . . . ," I revised my offer. "This is getting too big for me to handle by myself. Would you set that up for them? I'd really appreciate it." And I gave him Monroe's number.

Once we'd gotten that settled, Smitty started up again. "But Scuz, that's only half of what I called you about."

"You're kidding."

"Nope. This morning I took a drive by Horatio's gallery on Broadway. You'll never guess what I saw."

I couldn't and didn't.

"Fred must have some major pull with City Hall because the entire block between Ninth and Tenth has been barricaded off and they're setting up huge video monitors all along both sides of the street. I don't know exactly what they've got in mind but whatever it is, it's going to be BIG."

For some weird reason my mind flashed on a scene from a movie I'd seen years before in which the lead character hacked into a televised football transmission to broadcast his cheesy used car commercial.

"Say, Smitty," I asked, "you ever see that Kurt Russell movie—"

"Called *Used Cars*?" he finished my question. "Talk about simpatico ESP, compadre," he screamed in glee. "That's just what I was going to ask you."

Smitty then proceeded to tell me about his genius electronics buddy named "Laptop" and their plan to take over Fred's video feeds at the gallery opening the following night.

It seemed like a good idea at the time.

Chapter Thirty

I didn't realize I had a voice message on my cell phone until it chimed as I was pulling into my parking lot in the marina.

Can you hear me now? Probably not, I guessed.

"Dickhead." It was Ron Kimmel. "I've . . . a time . . . reaching yo . . . think . . . worked out now."

Yeah, it really sounded like it.

". . . in Tucson . . . Las Vega . . . home . . . onday."

This was ridiculous.

"But if . . . important . . . Thanks, pal."

Click.

I pushed the *return call* option.

"You've reached Ron's cell phone," his recorded greeting informed me. "If you're calling about the *Wedgies Gone Wild* video, you've got a wrong number."

Beep.

"Uh, yeah . . . (heavy breathing), I'm calling about the video. Just kidding. Hey Ron, it's Scuz. Call me on my cell."

Click.

All I wanted to do was take a nap.

But again, that was not to be, for the note on the hatch of my boat read, *Scott, I'll be at The Warehouse until 4:00. Let's talk. M.*

The Warehouse is a nautically themed restaurant an anchor's throw from my slip.

I looked at my watch—3:50.

It took me three minutes to cover the half-circle of sidewalk between my boat and where Marney was (hopefully still) waiting. As I came around the corner of the building and passed the Koi pond in the courtyard, she came walking out the front door.

As a general rule, I don't like facing up to situations that I'm trying to avoid. The fact that Marney and I arrived at the threshold of the restaurant at virtually the exact same time—like two comets colliding in space—only heightened the feeling.

"Uh . . . Marney," I stammered. "I got your note," stating the patently obvious.

But then she responded in kind. "I was just leav—" And stopped.

It was comforting to see we at least still had one thing in common.

"Want to go inside?" she motioned back toward the door from which she had just exited.

"Sure," I nodded for her to lead the way.

When we were at last seated on the waterfront patio, I couldn't help noticing anew just how fine she looked. So much so, in fact, that I found myself once again being thankful that my "innermost thoughts" weren't readable. However, when I finally wrenched my eyes up off her chest and onto her face, her not-too-amused smirk gave me pause to wonder.

"Scott, you really are a piece of work," she opened.

I didn't like the sound of that but I couldn't think of a response that would gain me anything, so I let it slide.

"I just got off the phone with Colleen and evidently she and Mort had a long discussion about the meeting you guys had today."

Long discussion? Exactly how fast did the female grapevine transmit information, anyway? I had left Mort . . . what? An hour ago? Now, I knew the Internet was invented by a guy. Women didn't need it.

"It appears you're not the backstabber I assumed you were."

I opened my mouth to respond, but, once again, a viable rebuttal didn't spring to mind, so I closed it and just tried to look "sympathetic" in the way that hotshot trial lawyers coach their mass-murdering clients to be.

At this point she became pensive and said nothing, but I knew better than to assume it was "my turn" to talk, so I continued to wait.

Tick-tock, tick-tock . . .

At last . . . she resumed speaking.

"The thing that upset me . . . ," her voice little more than a quivering whisper, "was the crack about me being a wannabe artist. Do you . . ." But then she halted, took an emotional dive for the worse and started to cry.

Damn, what was it with me lately? Did I have a *Cry to Me* sign on my forehead that I didn't know about?

Honk. Marney blew her nose into the linen napkin that our table setting provided. *Sniffle, sob, snort, snuffle.*

"Do you have any idea how long I've been trying to make it as a painter?" she at last "asked." Some "questions" are merely accusations worded in reverse, so I didn't attempt an "answer."

"I know what you're thinking," she then blurted out, suddenly angry.

She probably did, but since I wasn't entirely sure myself, I waited for her to fill me in.

"'Poor little rich girl.'" Her mouth took on a tauntingly cruel cast. "'Her daddy's money can't buy her success.'"

Well, I must admit, my *gast was flabbered*, as Archy McNally would say. Guys can get so used to women reading them like comic books that when one misses the mark, and widely, it's cause for genuine surprise.

"You can't possibly think . . . ," I began.

"Stop it," she yelped, her eyes getting into the act now too, turning all red and pooling with moisture. "*Stop it.* Don't you dare patronize me."

"Patronize?"

"Yes, patronize. You've got a career. You've worked hard for your success."

Her putting it that way made me feel pretty good but I didn't dare bask in it.

"What does that have to do with anything?" I finally got in my first fully formed sentence of the "conversation."

"You know what I mean," she shut me back down. "Everybody thinks the same thing."

Now it was "everybody."

"'She's Jack Eagleton's daughter.'"

I thought so.

"'She's rich. She doesn't have to work.'"

That's pretty rich.

"'She's got her life all laid out for her and all she's got to do is live it.'" With that, she started to bawl full-faced into her lap.

At this inopportune moment, our fresh-faced waiter arrived and asked, "Do we know what we want or do we still need a little more time?"

"Well, we've got it narrowed down to the salmon or the lobster bisque but my wife is still mulling it over," I responded with a somewhat apologetic expression on my face. "Could you give us a few more minutes? In fact, could you bring us two white wines and check back in an hour or so?"

At the prospect of serving "we" something, even if it was only a couple of wines, our waitperson brightened considerably. But just as he turned to fetch our order, Marney wailed into her napkin once more and he stopped short, stunned by her apparent angst over the menu.

"Don't mind her," I attempted to assuage his concern. "She's just not much on decisional situations."

"Oh?" He at first responded tentatively, looking at Marney then at me, quizzically. However, I gave him a reassuring look and after a moment or two he smiled cheerfully once again.

"Well, then I'll be right back with your wines." And he headed off in the direction of the bar.

Finally Marney honked one last time and looked up at me. Her face though flushed from crying, was amazingly sexy in a fresh-scrubbed kind of way. *God, men are such pigs*, I thought somewhat distractedly as the vast bulk of my attention was, once again, inexorably drawn down to her heaving breasts.

When I had at last completed my super-stealthy ogling and her face came back into focus, it became apparent that she was wrestling with something to say that for whatever reason was denying her a way to begin.

"Money is a funny thing," she finally said. "It's everywhere and nowhere, like happiness—a hard thing to keep around. When you're not in need, it comes and goes and overflows. But when you are, it can't be found."

Kind of poetic, I thought. Like that lyric from "Love Is a Rose," by Neil Young.

"But while the vast majority of popular press is devoted to the woes connected with the lack of money," Marney continued, looking at me now with an *I know you won't believe me, but it's true,* expression on her face, "the opposite case can be a problem too."

Won't believe her? I thought. Boy, she had me tagged correctly on that point. However, I willed my face into keeping the secret as best it could and waited for her to continue.

At length, she did.

"You see, you can get lulled into thinking it's a cure-all, when it's not. Money," she continued, "has become the universal prize, the carrot dangling from the stick held just out of reach in front of the donkey by the rider on its back."

That and sex, I thought. *Or is that just a guy thing?*

I couldn't remember the last time I was a female and had had a strong opinion one way or the other.

Whatever.

"It's . . . ," she clicked her lips and smiled wearily, "it's dreadful being broke. I'm not trying to discount that."

Well, that's good, I thought. *But I wouldn't have put it that way, exactly. How about* lousy *or* really the pits?

In fact, I found myself wondering whether she'd ever had any firsthand experience with not having enough money—such as being behind on the rent or having to put off getting her teeth fixed. Probably not.

"Without money," she added, "there's just no way you can be happy."

Well, I couldn't completely agree with her on that point either. At least as far as I was concerned.

Granted, I had seen lots of people get so tired of being unhappily broke that they eventually fixated on becoming happily wealthy.

Maybe that's what she was getting at.

"But just because one is wealthy . . . I mean, look at me. I've got all the money in the world and I still can't get arrested as an artist." Her eyes flashed. "How many pieces have I sold in the last . . . the last . . . ah hell, all year?"

I could identify with her there.

I thought about my miserable attempt to "make it" as a songwriter and how big a hole the failure had created in my life.

And as the saying goes, "Nature abhors a vacuum." So, of course, in poured all manner of shitty self-worth "issues," until at last I was walking around through life, more dead than alive.

Now that had been dreadful, to use Marney's word in a more appropriate context.

Maybe Marney could pull back from her artistic abyss and find another avenue for her creative spirit, like I had done with cabinetwork. It could happen. I found myself really hoping so.

"Is life really supposed to be this tough, this hard?" she voiced the question that she'd no doubt been struggling with for the last few minutes. "I mean, there's got to be a way to attain happiness without money being such a . . . ," she started, but didn't finish, instead, falling silent again. At length, she let her gaze sweep out onto the diamond-studded afternoon water.

Whoa. I thought. All this talk about "yenom" (as my friends and I used to call it) was starting to make my palms itch.

Had I sent the shop rent out? I wondered. I couldn't remember.

And that five hundred bucks I'd had to give Karl for my truck . . . that sure hadn't helped my happiness index this week.

I mean, I consider myself as empathetic as the next guy; however, I could feel myself really drifting on this conversation.

But then something occurred to me . . .

If Marney and I were ever really going to "bond," as they say—if we were ever really going to make it together—I was going to have to make a concerted effort to understand where she was coming from on this. There was no getting around it.

So I redoubled my effort to listen to what she was saying.

"Being happy," Marney finally declared, turning back to me, "that's all I've ever really wanted."

Man, I couldn't help myself from thinking. She could certainly join a nonexclusive club on that one.

And if that didn't work . . .

Oh, never mind.

"But the unfortunate fact is . . . ," she brushed a tear from her eye, smiling weakly, "like the old saying goes . . ."

I knew what she was going to say before she said it.

"Money can't buy you happiness."

Bingo. Trite, hackneyed, corny, but nevertheless, oh so wickedly true. And sometimes restating the obvious is the best way to put it.

"In fact . . . ," she looked conspiratorially at me, "I'm going to let you in on a little secret. A little secret that only great wealth, but especially—as in my case—only great, unearned wealth, can buy."

With that, she turned once again to look in silence out over the Marina.

Finally, after several seconds, she looked back at me and said, "When you really get right down to it, money, by itself, is just . . . just trash. It has no value of its own at all. It's not the big savior that everyone hopes it to be, needs it to be. In fact, it's got no other value than what you, yourself, bring to it."

With that, she dropped her gaze to her lap and started softly smoothing her hands, one with the other.

"And that's the cruelest joke of all." She sighed.

After half a minute or so, she looked up at me and added, "God, I hope you never have the misfortune to know what I'm talking about."

Then she started up again, crying softly to herself.

Corny or not, for the first time since suspecting Marney came from money—possibly for the first time ever—I found myself getting a glimmer of what she was talking about. And it was kind of depressing. For if money wasn't the big solution that all us peons thought it was—and someone with fifty million bucks ought to know—then what the hell was?

What the hell was? Indeed.

I was going to have to think about that some more.

Looking back on that conversation, if I had had to summarize the relationship that Marney and I had as a couple—I mean, right then, right at that exact moment—I would have had to say that our single biggest point of agreement was our love of esthetics (and sex, at least for me), and our single biggest point of disagreement was that she felt she was having problems with money while I felt I was having problems without it.

Maybe that was why rich people tended to marry other rich people and poor people marry other poor. Nobody else could understand them.

But be that as it may, whenever something in life really gets me snowed under and I lose sight of my own horizon—like with this conversation—I go surfing or sailing, or take a walk. I try to "get some space."

That's what I proposed to Marney. So we did.

At first we walked west on Admiralty out along the bike path, out toward the Venice pier. When we finally got there, we turned south and walked along the sidewalk bordering the sand and the alphabet streets until at last we reached the northern jetty of the marina.

By that time we were both feeling better. A lot better.

The sun was more down than up and though there was still a good hour of light left in the late August sky, the world had started to take on the aspect of early evening.

So we started back. By the time we finally made it to The Warehouse, the philosophical ramifications associated with art, money and happiness all seemed somehow to be more in perspective, more livable in scale. And that was a good thing—a fact that we could both wholeheartedly agree on.

It's funny the way life works with regard to understanding things. A little space (so that the thing you're trying to understand isn't pressing right up against your face) along with some light communication (so you can kick it around and look at it from different angles) goes a long, long way.

The same goes for understanding people.

The fact was that after our little walk and talk together, I felt Marney and I understood each other far better than we previously had.

Marney felt the same way.

When we at last reached her car, which had been parked in my lot since the night before, an additional life truth hit both of us: We were starving.

By the time we had brought a couple of burritos back to my boat and I had poured us a couple of beers, the sun had gone down completely and been replaced by a beautiful full summer moon. That being the case, we decided to sit up topside under the luminescent evening sky and enjoy our meal.

However, as Marney was setting out our plates, one of her breasts "accidentally" grazed my shoulder and I was again warmly reminded of just how sexy I thought she was.

I told her so.

"Oh Scott," she smiled coyly, her erect nipples casting diminutive shadows across the moonlit breastscape of her form-fitting T-shirt. "You have such a one-track mind."

Yeah, one-track, I thought, *and she's throwing all the switches.*

But what the hey, I wasn't proud. *All aboard.*

Some time later, our by then cold burritos tasted absolutely great.

Sunday

Chapter Thirty-One

I got up early the next morning and left Marney sleeping in the forward stateroom of my boat, while I drove over to get some coffee for the two of us.

On my way back—despite the first stirrings of a much-appreciated caffeine rush—I realized that I was still suffering from a hangover, philosophically that is, from last night's conversation with Marney.

As I said way back at the beginning of this story, I like philosophic answers. Answers, not questions.

A couple of things about Marney's diatribe on money still had me stymied.

So I sipped my coffee and mulled over the subject.

I hadn't driven two blocks before the heavens parted and I was struck with the obvious . . .

In our Western society, it's not only better to have money than not, it's mandatory. For while money, alone, might not secure one happiness, it sure can keep a lot of unhappiness at bay.

Furthermore, as long as the money is honestly come by—whether earned, inherited, found or won—the whole business about it being "deserved" or not is a bunch of hooey.

By all means, one should continue to work along his or her purposes to earn the happiness and sense of self-worth that only that can confer.

But, to beat oneself up for becoming inadvertently rich?

I say, use the money as constructively as one can. And leave it at that.

Marney could have just as well been born with flat feet, instead of an inheritance. Would she have "deserved" that?

I doubted it.

Of course, Marney was entitled to her own opinion otherwise, so I gave the subject a rest.

When I got back to the parking lot, Marney was climbing into her car.

"Hey, honey," I called out as I braked up alongside her with a chirp of rubber. "I got you some coffee. Didn't think you'd be taking off so soon."

"Oh thanks, Scott." She leaned back out and took the offered cup. "Yeah, I thought I'd get home and freshen up a bit." Smiling but then turning all business, she added, "Besides, if I'm going to round up tonight's key players for a noontime meeting at Colleen's, I'm going to have to get on it."

She was right, of course. The fact that I tend to procrastinate with regard to administrative duties was the exact reason why last night I'd asked her to help me take care of them.

"Oh and speaking of players . . . ," she continued, "Smitty and a guy named Laptop just dropped off the yearbook you wanted. They left it on the navigation table."

"Great," I said, looking longingly toward my boat and then back at her. "Is it as good as we hoped?"

"Even better." She smiled. "Our friend Freddie Blaire is all over that thing—quite the Big Man on Campus back then. And Bernie . . . you're not going to believe this. He played the lead in their production of *A Streetcar Named Desire.*"

"Whoa, that's a stretch. I can't wait to see it. Thanks for your help on this."

"Thanks, yourself." She leaned over and gave me a kiss on the cheek. "You're the one helping me, remember?" And with that, she swung back into her VW and fired up the engine.

With regard to my helping her, last night Marney had been very candid in relating what had happened after she had left the party with Bernard—fortunately, nothing had.

Long story short, Bernie hadn't had the nerve.

However, in spite of my telling her what might have happened if he had, it took my filling her in on some of what I had seen and heard about Feona's situation for Marney to finally realize how close she'd come.

And, more importantly, what bad news Horatio's whole operation was.

As I watched her pull out of the lot, my thoughts returned to *Streetcar*. For aside from it being one of the most magically lyrical titles for a piece of fiction ever coined, it had an oddly coincidental bearing on Marney's travails as an artist.

You see, it's been my experience that *Desire*—whether streetcar, bus, train, plane or boat—can be a very hit-or-miss form of locomotion, in terms of getting from point A to point B.

In other words, just because somebody wants something doesn't mean they're going to get it.

In fact, according to what I've seen—and here's the real switcheroo—it can happen that the more insistent one becomes in wanting something (you know, really having to have it), the more likely it is that that person is going to wind up not having it. Weird, but things just seem to work out that way.

I hoped Marney wouldn't end up going down that road with her art.

On the other hand, and sticking with the transportation theme, the only vehicle I'd ever seen that did reliably help in reaching one's dreams was a streetcar named *Interest.*

For while curiosity may kill cats, as the old saying goes, people are a different story. So much so in fact, that without a certain degree of curiosity, fascination or interest in one's address to living, "life" eventually becomes little more than a day-to-day slugfest of drudgery.

So, how does one achieve, retain or regain an interest in what one is doing? I don't entirely know, but that's an interesting question. I would have to get back to you on that.

At any rate, I made a mental note to talk with Marney about this possible approach to improving her career. It was worth a try.

As an additional aside on this, when I finally made the switch to being a successful cabinetmaker from failing as a songwriter, it was because I realized that I had an even wider purpose in life than to just write songs. And that was, to be involved with esthetics in general.

Spotting this finally unlocked my willingness to pursue another form of artistic expression. And I haven't looked back since.

Of course, I was fortunate at the time that I made the switch, because I had the help of Maurice in sorting this out. But nevertheless, I arrived at the realization myself by being interested enough to look for it. For what it's worth.

Chapter Thirty-Two

I drove back out to Ron's trailer a little early so I could have some time to myself before getting together with everybody at Colleen's.

After taking a shower and making something to eat, I still had an hour or so to kill, so I decided to walk up to Little Dume and check out what was left of the south swell that we had been enjoying.

As soon as I stepped out onto the sand, I could see that the swell was gone. Whereas just yesterday the humps of incoming waves, like a slow-moving freight train, had been visible for a couple of hundred yards out into the bay, today the surface of the water was like a lake.

And though the same sun shone down, seagulls wheeled and cried in the cloudless azure sky and the sand burned the bottoms of my bare feet—all as before—there was absolutely no surf.

Unless, of course, you could call the three-to-four inch "ankle slappers" that were "breaking" on the shoreline "surf." I couldn't.

Oh well, it was still a great day for a walk up the cove. So I headed out.

I don't know whether it was my preoccupation with the upcoming meeting at Colleen's, the lack of a compelling swell to keep my attention focused outward or just the sun that had lulled me into sort of a walking siesta, but I didn't see Weegee until I was right up on him.

"*Cómo estás*, Scuz?" Weegee said softly. His greeting brought me out of my reverie, a state I hadn't even known I had been in.

"Weegee," I managed to say, stopping abruptly and trying to regain my bearings.

"I was going to wait to see if you'd actually walk right into me, before I said anything." He grinned a sunny grin. "But I changed my mind at the last second."

"Thanks." I smiled sheepishly. "I guess I've got a lot on my mind."

"No harm, no foul." And then, looking out onto the perfectly placid water, he said, "Bummer about the swell, huh?"

"Yeah, it was a good one," I said. Looking out onto the water now myself, "Short-lived, though."

"Yep," he responded somewhat distantly, the warmth of the sun and the hypnotic beauty of the ocean casting a spell over both of us now, just standing in silence and surveying the bay.

Living near the water does something to your sense of time. The ocean, with all its moods, is at once constantly changing, but on the other hand, eternally unchanged.

This day was, of course, itself unique, but I couldn't

help feeling it was the same as every other day that I'd stood on the shore under a late summer sun—over twenty late summer suns now—and wondered if there would still be one more south swell before the cold winter waves started coming down from the north.

The changing seasons—endings and new beginnings—what are you going to do? It's the way things are, but it's always filled me with a sort of sadness.

"So, you leaving for school soon?" I asked Weegee.

"Oh, didn't you hear?" He perked up. "Mom's gonna homeschool me this year," the ocean's spell over him broken at the thought of his new adventure. "I'm really looking forward to it."

"That's . . . that's a big change," I responded, sounding more equivocal than I felt.

I'm not a fan of the way public schools conduct their business these days and even most private schools are deficient, in my opinion, so it wasn't much a matter of "love lost" on that account.

No, I guess I was just hoping that whatever Weegee's educational situation was, he and his mom got it sorted out.

"What made her decide to do that?" I asked.

"It was kind of a . . . I don't know . . . a mutual decision, you could say."

Then, apparently concerned that maybe home-schooling did hold a negative connotation for me, he asserted, "She's going to do a great job, I know." Giving me a sidelong glance now, small worry lines forming around his eyes, "She's really good with reading and, you know, whatever you're supposed to do in school."

"I'm sure she is," I said earnestly. But sensing his

still lingering discomfort and doubt, I mustered as much confidence into a smile as I could and said, "I'm sure you two are going to do great together. I really mean it."

That seemed to ease his mind because suddenly his face lit up and he nearly shouted his next piece of news.

"You know what else! (It wasn't a question.) She's going to teach me to be a writer," facing me fully now, his young body humming with excitement.

Now that was unexpected news.

"A writer. Really?"

"Yeah, she said she'd show me the ropes. It could even count as credit toward my classes. And I've already come up with a title for a book," he exclaimed.

"Yeah? What is it?"

"*Bungee Cords of Love.*" He waited breathlessly for me to respond.

Bungee . . . Cords . . . I could hear the cogs grinding but I couldn't get my thoughts into gear.

"Bungee?" I finally choked out.

"Yeah, bungee cords. Like you use to tie surfboards on top of your car," he explained, his enthusiasm for the project more than compensating for my current lack of participation in the conversation. "Don't you see?" his excitement mounting even higher, "a passion so strong, it's like the two young lovers in the story are held together with bungee cords."

Two . . . young . . . lovers? I thought. This was a side of Weegee I hadn't seen before.

Just where, and from whom, is he getting his newfound "inspiration"? I wondered.

It was then that I saw her, angling down the beach toward us. I say "toward us" for there was no one else on this part of the beach but us, and the young girl (woman-child?) was walking with such resolute purpose in our direction that it was impossible to conceive that she had any other destination in mind, save for Weegee and me. Er . . . make that Weegee.

Weegee must have sensed my attention off over his shoulder, because he turned around just as she closed in on the last twenty yards that separated us.

"Raney," he yelped happily and loped off to greet her.

Two young lovers, I thought.

Raney, as Weegee had called her, was every inch as tall as he was, rail thin and all angles—the way newborn fawns are.

He would have kissed her when they met if I hadn't been present, I'm sure. But since I was, he guided her gently toward me for what I assumed would be a brief round of introductions.

As amused and "mature" as I had begun to feel at witnessing this touchingly innocent vignette of "young love" playing out before me, I was literally stunned into disbelief when Raney was at last truly within eyesight. For she had an aura of grace about her that was beyond . . .

Well, let's see . . . Her face . . . How can I describe it?

Cheekbones, high and hollow . . . the delicate line of her jaw . . . a finely proportioned nose . . .

"Scott." It was Weegee speaking to me from what seemed like miles away. "I'd like you to meet Raney." Then, looking at her and motioning to me, "Raney, this is Scott."

"I'm pleased to meet you, Scott," Raney smiled. The affinity radiating naturally off her like a pleasant sun could have warmed a small village . . . in the dead of winter . . . on the dark side of the Arctic.

"Ah . . . er . . . uhhh . . . ," I responded.

"Scott's his grown-up name," Weegee informed her. "But you can call him Scuz, if you want."

"Well, that's even better." She smiled another planet-warming smile. "I'm pleased to meet you, Scuz."

"Er . . . uh . . . ah . . . hi," I finally got the word out.

God, I thought, *does it never end?* Just when I thought I had accumulated to myself a certain amount of *je ne sais quoi*—you know, poise, or grace in the presence of the fairer sex—here I was yet again, reduced to rubble.

Mercifully, Raney didn't seem to notice, or if she did, didn't seem to hold it against me.

Then, as Weegee stood facing me, beaming with a tremendously pleased and proud expression on his face, Raney, with the lightest and most subtle of touches, brushed the back of her hand against his bare midriff and said a bit breathlessly, "I'll let you guys finish up, but remember . . . ," looking at Weegee now, "you promised to go surfing with me today." And she did that earth-warming thing again with her smile.

I flicked my vision out onto the water to see if by some miracle the swell had suddenly returned while Weegee and I hadn't been looking.

Nope.

Schwing. When I looked back at Weegee, his nipples had turned as hard as a couple of marbles, his complete upper torso had become mottled with goosebumps and his swimming trunks suddenly seemed to fit him a bit tighter.

Both Weegee and I watched silently as Raney gracefully traversed the distance between the hot, dry sand, where we stood, and the cool, wet sand of the waterline where the tiny wavelets were rippling ashore.

"She's amazing, isn't she?" It was Weegee speaking, but it could just as well have been me.

"My God, Weegee, where on Earth did you meet her?"

"She lives out here. On Grayfox, just up from us."

"But, how . . . who is she?"

"Her dad's a producer." He shrugged his shoulders, as if shaking off his own disbelief at his great good fortune. "And her mom's an actress."

"Producer?"

"Yeah, TV. You know that show Bamboozled?"

Bamboozled, I thought, but I couldn't place it. So I let my mind drift off to TV Land to take a better look—where Archie, and The Beav, Hawkeye and Lovejoy were all still alive and well.

"You know . . ." It was Weegee speaking, as if in voice-over, atop one of my favorite episodes of Maverick. "*WHAM.*"

"Huh?"

"*BAM.*"

"Whaa?"

"*BOOOOZZZZLED.*"

"Wham, bam, what?" I asked, suddenly back from the past.

"It's their, you know, gimmick. The thing everybody yells when they burst in on whoever they're filming that week. Their . . . their . . . It's a reality show. Their . . ." Weegee was reaching, but not connecting.

"You mean *catch phrase*?" I asked.

"Yeah, that's it. *Wham-Bam-Booozzzled.*"

Now that he mentioned it, I had seen the promos on

TV, starring the young, hunky actor-turned-reality show practical jokester. And yes, he was married to an older but still phenomenally boob-a-licious actress. What was her name?

"Well, anyway . . ." It was Weegee, again.

I looked up to see him slowly stepping back toward where Raney stood patiently watching some diving gulls.

"I've got to catch up with my . . . with Raney." And he rolled his eyes in her direction as if his words might possibly need clarification.

"Yeah . . . uh, Weegee . . . ," I said, stopping his steps backward with my words. "I'm happy for you."

"Thanks," he said.

But just as he was turning to go, I added, "Don't forget. If you go surfing, that is. Don't forget to wear . . . to wear a wetsuit."

For a second he didn't get what I meant, but then a big, appreciative smile settled across his entire face.

"Thanks, Scuz," he said, giving me a double-handed thumbs-up. "Catch you later." And he ran off to join Raney.

Chapter Thirty-Three

As I approached Colleen's place in my truck, I was having second thoughts about my plan to deal with Fred Blaire.

I had originally thought that getting a whole bunch of people together to show up at his gallery opening and somehow "embarrassing" him would be the way to go. However, the closer tonight's party had loomed, the less confident I'd become that this strategy would indeed succeed.

Why? Because a guy like Blaire doesn't "embarrass" well.

He doesn't "guilt" well, either.

No, the unfortunate fact was that even though Fred had gone to great lengths to cultivate the image of an urbane gallery owner, it was highly unlikely that publicly disclosing his "hayseed" provenance—as I had at first imagined—would slow him down one bit.

He'd just steamroll right over it.

Besides—and this was probably more to the point—aren't most of us trying to reinvent and better our situations one way or another, anyway? Certainly, there's no foul there. Not even for the Horatio Blaires of the world.

But Fred had crossed the line. "Better for him" had become for the most part, "worse for everyone else."

Therefore it was clear to me that I was going to have to dig a little deeper than his farm boy roots if I was going to gain any leverage over the situation.

Since surrendering to this conclusion, I had come up with two possible alternative approaches. To wit:

A. To "out" Fred's clients as frequenting prostitutes (messy and really not hitting at Fred directly, as he could always accumulate more), or
B. To broadly expose Fred as being the backstabbing psycho-dog that he truly was.

I had chosen the second strategy but still hadn't figured out how I was going to pull it off.

This notwithstanding, the factors of public relations, intelligence, security and technical support while at the party remained spheres of valid concern and ones that a large number of people "on our side" would be indispensable in handling. So I pressed on toward Colleen's.

When I finally arrived at her place, or should I say, finally arrived within a couple of hundred yards of her house, both sides of Grayfox were lined with vehicles—limos, beemers, Bentleys, MBZs, Porsches, 'vettes, Hummers, customized SUVs, rice rockets, woodies, choppers, hot rods, exotics and even some electric golf carts. It seemed not only did nature abhor a vacuum, but so did a party in Malibu, formal or otherwise.

I snagged the first parking spot I could find, and when I walked around the bend into Colleen's driveway, I was greeted with another tangle of personal conveyances—skateboards, bicycles, go-peds and a couple of those stupid, two-wheeled, "I'm so rich I don't have to walk," human-lawnmower-looking contraptions I'd started seeing more of around L.A.

The word had definitely gotten out. Hundreds of people had filled the inside of Colleen's modest ranch-style home. The "backyard" (overlooking the ocean), now also full, had begun to overflow into the front and side yards.

My first instinct was to turn and leave as I'm really not into large crowds. However, word of my impending arrival and, no doubt, "importance" to what was happening, had evidently preceded me, for all at once a voice boomed above the buzz and boil of the crowd.

"*Yo eva body,* make room fo the *S-Man.*"

It was Maize N J.

"My brotha," he gushed.

Swivel hip, head drape, sleepy smile, *checkin'.*

"Long time, no visio."

Funny, it just seemed like yesterday, to me. However, in spite of that little discrepancy, I found myself being seduced by the moment as he worked me through a handshake routine that topped anything Weegee had ever put me through.

"S'apnin', Maize," I said (I can sound cool too, when I want to).

"Dis be . . ." And then Maize N J motioned to three incredibly bored-looking girls in halter tops, short shorts and 4 inch red stilettos. "Seesha, Keesha and Fleesha."

Their names had the remote ring of some kind of obscure warning, but I couldn't quite make it out it before he continued.

"N Difference," he announced with what seemed to be fatherly pride. "I'm producin' their next CD."

Shoulder roll, arm fling, hand dangle, *checkin'*.

"Gonna be big," he informed me modestly. "Called *Safe and Sexy*—single be 'Trojan Horse.'" Maize winked, *mano à mano*. "Nationally known condom manufacturer, picking up the tab for the recordin' costs."

Checkin'.

"Yeah, it be sweet." He drifted off thinking about it, a big smile on his pimply white face. Then popping out of his reverie, "I'll call you when we have the wrap party." And he handed me off to the next person in the gauntlet, leading toward Colleen's living room.

Now I knew what Brad Pitt must feel like.

"Hi Scu-uz." The words dripped like honey off the lips of a girl who looked like trouble. "Wanna BJ?"

Before I could answer, a disembodied voice yelled out over the crowd. "SCUZ. What the hell you doing hanging outside for?"

It was Smitty.

"We've been waitin' for you."

By the time I finally reached the innermost sanctum *sanctorum*—Colleen's writing room—I felt like what Mötley Crüe must have felt like when they used to throw those house parties above the Sunset strip. Everybody I had passed en route had wanted a piece of me—a touch, a shred of my shirt, my bodily fluids.

"Scott. Thank God." It was Colleen, calling to me from the far side of the room. "We were starting to worry you weren't going to make it," she said, relief now noticeably softening her features.

"I . . ." But I just let it go, and said instead, "Where in the name of Samuel L. Goldwyn did all these people come from?"

"You're asking me?" Colleen exclaimed. "They started showing up at ten this morning. I had to call Andy Gump to get some porto-potties out here. Those and a couple of taco wagons from Chico's. They better get here soon or . . . ," the worry lines etching themselves back into her face.

"Now, now, honey." It was Mort at her side, comforting her.

I hadn't seen him when I'd first entered the room, but then I'd been in such a state of shock that I hadn't seen anyone.

Now that my racing heart was finally starting to normalize, I looked around the room and took inventory of who else was there.

Smitty, of course. Marney, Feona and Monroe. Pole, *good.* And over in the corner, sort of hanging back like a bat out of the light, a pasty-looking guy who I could only assume was Smitty's pal, Laptop.

"Where's Weegee?" I asked of no one in particular.

"Oh, he called and said he was going surfing with his new girlfriend." It was Marney speaking. "Said he'd catch up with us later tonight."

Ride, ride, ride the wild surf, I thought.

"Well, it looks like he's already done what he said he was going to do," I said, scanning the faces of everybody assembled. "So let's get down to business."

With that, I told them the good news: the Fresno State yearbook; Feona's testimony to me (without getting into specifics); the fact that Pole was going to help us as an "inside man" once we made contact with Horatio; Monroe and his posse from the record label; and how Smitty had lined up the two girls who used to be on Fred's cheerleading squad.

And then I told them the bad: In spite of all we had in terms of "embarrassing background" on Fred, I still thought—in fact I was certain—that it wasn't going to be enough to derail him. By the time I had finished, the room had taken on a somber silence.

"But what about going to the police?" It was Feona. "I'd be willing to file a complaint."

"And ruin your career?" I played devil's advocate. "Your life story would be on every tabloid and TV gossip show faster than you could empty out a red carpet with a dog turd. We're not going to go there." And then, easing up on her a bit, I said, "I'm sorry, but thanks for offering."

"How 'bout what we can do?" It was Monroe, weighing in sensibly.

"All right, let's look at that," I said.

So I ran down my ideas about deploying our own security people at the party, in case things got out of hand; having our own technical guys to tap into the communication and video feeds that Fred had set up; organizing another group to keep us abreast of any intelligence issues; and finally a group of us to put the right spin on things if and when we did finally gain control of Fred's party.

After twenty minutes or so, we had a pretty good handle on everything that had to be done and who was in charge of it.

Laptop had even set all of us up with tiny communication sets that fit into our ears. In fact—

probably because he didn't get out much himself and wanted to feel like a "player"—he took me aside and rigged me up with an additional microphone that was, as he put it, "completely off the grid." Whatever that meant.

Everything was taken care of.

Everything, except how we were actually going to get rid of Fred. And despite considerable additional discussion, that subject proved remarkably unfruitful in terms of a solution. That is, until Pole, who had been hanging back throughout most of this, cleared his throat and said, "I think I've got an idea."

When he was done with his presentation—although the plan seemed extraordinarily simple—I had to admit, *It just might work.*

After kicking it around amongst ourselves some more without being able to come up with anything better, I at last said, "All right. Well, I guess that's it," and looked at Pole. "It'll be just you and me on the actual grab, so we better watch each other's back."

"Got that right," the Brit agreed soberly. "But as God is my witness . . . ," he paused, slowly making eye contact with each person in the room, until he was finally looking back at me. "I'll deliver him to you. And when I do . . . ," he smiled evilly, "there'll be hell to pay."

Well, all right. Let's party.

Chapter Thirty-Four

"OK, let's try this," I said into my tiny microphone.

I was standing on Broadway, about a block west from where it had been barricaded off for Fred's opening. The rest of my "platoon" was scattered out around the entire remaining perimeter of the party—north, east and south.

It was 10:00 P.M. and things were just getting going.

"Beagle Two, this is Beagle One, do you copy?"

"Yes, Beagle One, this is Beagle—" It was Monroe.

"Hey, I thought I was Beagle Two," exclaimed Marney.

"No, Marney," I corrected, "you're Beagle Four, Monroe is Beagle Two"

"Well, I could have sworn I was . . . ," Marney's voice trailed off.

"That's fine, Marney. Let's do that again," I responded, trying to keep the irritation I was starting to feel from seeping into my voice.

"OK, from the top. Beagle Two, this is Beagle—"

"Uh, Scott," Mort cut in, "am I still Beagle Six? I'd rather be the fifth Beagle." He was giggling.

"I'll take a beagle with cream cheese." It sounded like Smitty.

"Quiet," I yelled. "You guys aren't taking this seriously enough. Just shut the hell up so we can get through this, OK?"

Dead silence enveloped our entire network for about ten seconds, but just as I was about to try it again, Smitty opened up once more.

"Beagle, Beagle One-Niner, this is Yogi Beagle, do you read? Can you read? If so, can I look at the centerfold when you're done?"

At first I could hear snickers coming from various sources in my earpiece, but then, gradually, more and more members of the crew started piling on until the snickers filled in and became giggles, which in turn became chuckles, and then, at length, out-and-out laughter, which started building . . . and building . . . until at last raucous amusement, punctuated with guffaws, hoots, belly laughs and squeals, was all that could be heard throughout our private little closed-circuit communication system.

In short, my earpiece sounded like a bunch of cub scouts telling jokes in a pup tent, way, way, *way* past the time that they're all supposed to be asleep.

"OK, OK, *OK,*" I shouted into my microphone. "Forget the Beagles. We're not doing the Beagles anymore. To hell with the Beagles."

Silence reigned once more up and down the entire length and breadth of our audio domain.

"Marney?"

"Yeah."

"Mort?"

"Here, and so is Colleen. In fact, Weegee was here a minute ago, too."

"Monroe?"

"Got you covered."

"And Feona?

"With me." It was Monroe again.

"OK. Smitty?"

"Yo."

"Laptop?"

"That's a Roger."

More snickers, probably from Smitty or Mort.

"Pole?"

No response.

"*Pole?*"

"Uh, yeah, sorry. Got your back."

"All right," I said with an air of confidence that I didn't feel in the slightest. "Let's move in and assume our positions." And then for the hell of it, I closed, "The Beagle has landed, over and out."

Click.

Fear sets in when most everything that you have been counting on to see you through a crisis begins to fail or seems inadequate. Now as I stood and looked east up Broadway toward the party, the solace I had drawn from our seemingly well-laid plan just hours earlier in the safety of Colleen's home had started to evaporate. My comrades-in-arms, with whom I had shared a last moment of mutual courage and confidence earlier, were no longer with me.

In fact, the very reason why I had first decided to do what I was finally doing, once so clear and emphatic, now seemed somehow vague and open to question. And in the place of these comforts—and anything else I could think of that might help me feel more confident—resided only cold, numbing seeds of fear, which had started to sprout and grow.

Now, I've spent much of this story pontificating or holding forth on "truth"—philosophical truth. This has all been very well and good as far as it has gone, and the things I have espoused have indeed been true. However, there is another type of truth that I haven't talked about. And that's the truth of whether or not one has the courage to do what one has set out to do when the time arrives to finally do it.

Of these two expressions of truth, I believe the latter is the greater. For courage is a manifestation of the truth of the person himself. It can't be written down or symbolized. It has to be lived.

And because of that fact, it is uniquely different for every single individual who soars, walks or crawls through this life. For this truth is a decision, a response . . .

"Am I going to do this, see this through? Or, am I not?" That is the question. And the answer that one settles on is probably the only truth in the entire universe that matters to an individual in the final analysis.

I don't like this fact (if indeed it is one) because I'm not a hero, nor do I particularly want to be—I don't stand out in a crowd, and that's the way I like it.

But in spite of my distaste for it, this is the way I look at things. Because it keeps things simple for me, keeps things from getting out of hand.

And so, having made my decision, settled on my answer, I headed east up Broadway toward the bright lights of the party.

The plan that we had finally adopted had been simple. While Smitty, Feona, Monroe, Colleen, Marney and Laptop all kept an eye out for Fred from the north and south sides of Broadway, Pole would start walking from the east end of the party heading west and I would proceed from the west end, heading east.

Once Blaire was spotted, Pole would move in to keep him occupied while I snuck up on his blind side. When Pole and I finally had Fred subdued, the rest of the crew would converge on him as well. At this point, we'd all threaten to kick the shit out of him unless he turned over the pictures of Feona and left town.

OK. Now I know what you're thinking. And no, I'm not a moron.

Because you see, Pole and I and everybody else went around and around on this at Colleen's place. And we finally decided that no matter how lofty and reasonable my idea had seemed about "broadly exposing Fred as a back-stabbing psycho-dog," we were all fairly certain that we probably wouldn't be able to pull that off.

So, we had at last settled on the plan that I've just outlined.

And again, no, I'm not a moron.

In fact, in my defense, if you want to reread the part of the last chapter that applies to this, I said Pole's idea was a simple plan, not a good one, just a simple one. So, there.

And the plan was indeed simple. Perhaps overly so. That may account, at least in part, for why it immediately started to fail. For the absolute second I crossed the barricade into the party area, a gorilla-timbered voice off behind my left shoulder about two feet away asked me, "You Scuzman?"

I don't know about you, but I don't particularly feel induced, enticed or encouraged to respond to people in the dark who are big and scary and are asking me whether or not I am who I am. To the contrary, I mostly feel in situations like this that it might in fact be better to pretend to be someone other than myself.

So I said nothing.

Then, off to my right, I heard a second gorilla speak.

"Yeah, Lenny. (Heavy breathing) It sure looks like 'im."

The term "vise grip" conjures up the descriptive concept that corresponds to the actual pain I felt in my left bicep as Lenny grabbed hold of me. Seconds later, I lost sensation in the adjacent lower arm and hand.

When Lenny's pal, "Big Al" – I think I overheard Lenny call him that - grabbed my right bicep to form the second bookend of pain that I now found myself bracketed between, I almost "sharted," like Philip Seymour Hoffman's character did in that movie, *Along Came Polly*. Then I passed out for a minute or so.

Anyway, when I regained consciousness, I was walking on my tiptoes around the perimeter of the party where all the generators, party supplies and behind-the-scenes personnel were hurrying and scurrying in the performance of their duties and chores.

I say "walking on my tiptoes" because the toes of my feet were indeed making contact with the ground—but only about every five or ten feet. For you see, the vast bulk of my vertical support and forward locomotion was being furnished by Lenny and Big Al, who were still holding my arms in their beefy hands. Really not good.

We walked in this manner with no questions asked or explanations offered for what seemed like one hundred and fifty feet, until we at last came to a big aluminum trailer like the kind they use on location shoots to house and dress actors.

Lenny knocked on the flimsy-sounding door (under his pummeling) and this at length elicited a muted grunt from the inside of the trailer.

"Got the package," Lenny announced, at which point the trailer door swung open and I was momentarily blinded by the light that washed over me from inside.

With Lenny and Big Al's "help," I bounded in one the three steps leading into the trailer's interior, crossed the twelve-foot expanse of the little room without so much as touching a toe to the floor and "sat down" in the leather couch that was positioned against the far wall.

The other big guy, the one who had opened the door for us, took up a sentinel position standing at the left end of the couch that I now occupied.

It took me a few seconds but when the blood circulation finally began to return to my arms and hands with an excruciating tingle, I realized that Lenny and Big Al were no longer holding on to me. They too had taken up positions, arms crossed like a couple of buffaloes, one on either side of the door I had just come through, and were staring stonily straight ahead at nothing at all.

OK, Mr. Philosophy, I thought, *what're you gonna do now?*

I was mulling this over when, out of my right eye, peripherally, I saw someone enter the room.

"Hey mate." It was Pole.

"Oh God, I am so glad to see you," I said, and started to get up off the couch.

"And I you," he said, crossing the room toward me, extending his right hand out as if to shake my hand.

But his hand kept on going and . . . *POW.* Right into my jaw.

I "sat" back down, but on the floor this time.

"Whaa thaa faa?" I asked.

"Yeah, I know what you mean, but let's take care of some business here first, why don't we." And he leaned over, unceremoniously ripped the tiny communication set from my ear, dropped it to the floor and ground it into the linoleum with the heel of his boot. "Now, what were you saying?"

I had forgotten.

"Oh well, if you remember, let me know." And he smiled that same evil smile he had at Colleen's.

Fear is a "funny" thing. It's mostly a state of mind where you want to flee and your thoughts tend to flee from you as well. But one thought, one moment from the past, came clearly and fully to mind.

Yeah, he's got nothing to lose. It had been Feona who had told me that yesterday morning, when I asked her whether Pole would go along with our plan to bring down Fred and Bernie. *The money's been good for him, no doubt, but he can't stand either of them,* she had said.

And then a nagging series of thoughts I had been having all along—but not having, if you know what I mean—finally came into focus . . .

If Pole "had nothing to lose," and his own self-portraits certainly ruled out the possibility that he was being photographically blackmailed, why had he stayed with the gallery? That is, if he had wanted to leave?

There would have been nothing to hold him captive in the way that there had been with Feona.

The other niggling detail had been what Pole himself had said to me that first night at the preview party . . .

All's I can say is, ever since I connected up with them two blokes, my work's been selling like bloody 'otcakes and I'm driving a Jag, 'stead of a Ford Escort.

So there you go. Better late than never, I guess.

But I didn't have time to work up a big head of cheer about it because at that exact moment, Fred Blaire came walking through a door to my right that I hadn't noticed before, idly thumbing through the pages of his alma mater's yearbook.

Oh God.

Pole had been looking at that book this afternoon.

And then things started to really tumble down in my mind: Fred knew everything. I was truly and, indeed, fully screwed.

And so were all my friends, for all I knew.

Shit on a shingle.

At the sound of Fred's entrance, Pole at first looked over his shoulder at him and then looked back at me.

"See?" Pole said, smiling that weird-ass smile of his. "Promise kept."

"Promishh?" I asked.

"Yeah, at Colleen's today," he replied, looking at me, wanting me to remember. "I promised I'd deliver Fred to you." The smile again—I was really getting sick of his smile. "And here he is."

"And then I promised," he continued, smiling at Fred now, "there'd be hell to pay. Well, guess what?" he asked, looking at me once more. "Welcome to hell. It's payback time."

"I thought you hated Fred?" I blurted stupidly.

"Oh he does, dear boy." It was Fred now. And with that, he glided over to Pole's side, tilted Pole's head back and kissed him fully, voraciously, on the lips. When he finally came up for air, Fred said, "Pole hates everybody." He winked at Pole and then turned to smile at me. "That's part of his charm."

Shit, shit, shit.

I didn't hear the door open again, or even see Bernie come through it. All I know is one second he wasn't in the room, the next, he was.

He looked at my lip, which I was fairly sure was now pretty swollen, winced a bit and nervously shrank back into a corner to watch.

"Take my bandanna," Fred began singing to himself in a soft, crooning warble, "and catch all those crocodile tears."

And then he nodded at Pole.

WHAM. Another shot to my head.

"You better save them, for someone who cares," Fred teased, bopping his head in time to a shit-kickin' song only he could hear. "And wipe off that shattered look . . . ," winking at Pole.

"Uhhh." I flinched in terror. But it had only been a fake.

". . . you've got on your face."

BAM. A sucker punch I hadn't seen coming at all.

"That's one expression . . . ," Fred kneeled down now to where I was fully on the floor, and whispered, "you don't want to waste." Then he stood up.

Tell me this isn't happening.

"'Cause I know a good thing . . . ," he turned as if to leave me alone, "when it's walkin' away." But then he suddenly wheeled back and kicked me hard in the ribs. "And it's a good, good thing . . . ," and he kicked me again, "that you're leaving today."

Personally, I liked the Kadota Figs' version of the song better and I would have told Fred so, but I didn't think I could get my mouth to work, so I let it go.

"So now that I've got your attention, Skuzman . . ." Fred leaned back down to where his face was just inches from mine. "I do have your attention, don't I?"

"Uhh."

"Pole here tells me you think my little art business—oh what the hell, we're among friends here—prostitution ring, shouldn't be allowed to continue to service all the moneyed and pervy residents of Beverly Park. Says that you object to my blackmailing Karizma, or Feona, as you so fondly refer to her. In fact, that you'd like to turn all my johns . . . er, clients, against me." And then he started to laugh softly to himself.

"Only trouble is, you're a little late for that. You see, even if you did manage to convince some of my clients to turn against me, I've got them all photographed eight ways to Sunday. And I don't mean Sunday school.

"No, as detestable as this operation may seem to you now, it's only phase one. You have no idea how much merchandise I'm going to be moving and money I'm going to be making once I start letting word slip out amongst all my upstanding art patrons that I have more pieces of art, quote unquote, that they would rather not have hanging on their walls, than I do that they would."

Then he started to laugh a weird maniacal laugh.

"Game's over, dipshit." And he turned to Pole and said, "Take him out to the desert and kill him."

"WHAAAM."

The whole room lit up.

"BAAAM."

God, I saw stars.

"BOOOOOZZZLED."

And all hell broke loose—voices shouting, bodies flying, furniture breaking.

I think I even heard a gun go off, but I couldn't be certain because I was back there with the Figs, singing . . .

"I'm glad to be off your lovin'-go-'round
There's too many ups and downs.
You've threatened to leave me so many times
So leave me, I'm holdin' my ground.
'Cause I know a good thing, when it's walkin' away.
Yeah a good thing, when it's walkin' away.
So be a good, good thing . . .
And keep walkin' away."

Monday (Labor Day)

Chapter Thirty-Five

I didn't get released from UCLA Medical until about 4:00 A.M.—Labor Day weekend being one of the busier of the year.

But be that as it may, the good news was I didn't have any broken ribs or bones.

The bad news, hmmm . . .

Come to think of it, there wasn't any. I was just so very happy to be alive.

And the news kept getting better on the drive back to Paradise Cove as Marney, Colleen, Weegee and Mort all vied to fill me in on what had happened the night before.

Long story, compressed . . .

The additional dedicated microphone/GPS beacon that Laptop had planted on me had saved the day.

Weegee's connection through Raney had sent the *Bamboozled* crew bursting in on Fred, Pole and me at the last possible moment, saving my ass and documenting the entire scene for future litigation and entertainment (slated to air the first week of TV's fall season—pending the D.A.'s approval, of course).

The giant video screens scattered throughout the party area (which Laptop had commandeered for us) had transmitted the blow-by-blow *Bamboozled* encounter with Fred, Pole and the boys to not only the local partygoers, but across the planet as well (the highlights were no doubt bouncing off satellites and careening through modems already).

Fred, Pole, Bernie and the goon squad had all been arrested and were facing some serious prison time.

Feona had retrieved her blackmail pictures from Fred's studio and sold a ton of her own work at the opening.

Fred's client base of, as he had put it, "art patrons," had receded into the woodwork and probably wouldn't be resurfacing anytime soon.

Oh, and Ron Kimmel had called about 11:00 P.M. and said that he would be home Monday (today). Well, this last about Ron wasn't the best of news, for I had begun to feel a bit like a "local" on the Malibu scene these last . . . *God* . . . had it only been four days?

But, all in all, it was a great big bundle of good news with a bright red ribbon tied around it. And I liked that.

I liked that a lot. In fact, I fell asleep in the car thinking so.

Chapter Thirty-Six

Later that day, Ron Kimmel sauntered out onto the deck of his home where Marney, Mort, Colleen and I lay, soaking up the sun.

"Who's the fag?" he asked of no one in particular, motioning to Mort languishing in his flamboyant, electric watermelon-green Speedos.

Without missing a beat, Colleen rolled up on one elbow, facing down over Mort, and grabbed a handful of his "electric melon" with her free hand.

"Hello." His eyes shot wide with surprise, but then, recognizing Colleen's smiling face inches above his, he pulled her mouth down and kissed her for a long time.

"Oh," noted Ron, and headed back into the relative gloom of the trailer.

Ronald Fulbright Kimmel III—Mr. "Live and let live." *He could be a real asshole sometimes*, I mused as the throaty growl of his Porsche barked to life somewhere out back.

"Hey, honey." It was Marney rising up over me to her feet. "I think we better, you know . . . ," she said, motioning to Mort and Colleen with her head.

I looked over at the still embracing couple and finally said, "Yeah, I guess you're right," trying to summon the strength for the long haul up.

"Say . . . ," a playful perkiness suddenly infused Marney's face, "did I ever show you my etchings?" And she blushed slightly.

I thought about her question for a second and then smiled a somewhat perky smile of my own.

"Itchings? You've got itchings?"

"That," she said, smiling broadly now, "I do." And she reached down to give me a hand up.

That night, Marney and I walked up the cove toward Little Dume. The full moon had just risen above Palos Verdes and was still low enough that it appeared to be half again its normal size. A light breeze ruffled the surface of the ocean and the moon's reflection on it looked like a *bling* highway leading due south all the way across the Santa Monica bay.

"Pretty nice, huh?" I said.

"Doesn't get much better," she murmured, snuggling closer to me. "You know, somehow," she continued, "I knew that first night, when I saw you and Ron drive to the airport, that we would end up like this."

"Umm." I smiled into the crook of her neck, our arms around each other now, standing in the sand. "That *night.*" My head jerked upright and my mind began racing. "You mean, the next morning at Ron's trailer wasn't the first time you laid eyes on me?" Holding her loosely at arm's length now, "My God. That means my theory concerning chance flirtatious encounters just might be—"

"Scuzman," Marney cut me off, smiling knowingly. "Ride the wave."

And we did.

About the Author

Frank Brian lives just outside of Los Angeles with his wife and family. "Riding the Wave" is his first novel. He is currently completing work on its sequel. He's also the author of the non-fiction weight-loss eBook entitled, "Fat Wanker No More."

Published by Pacifican Books

To purchase additional copies of this book, or other books by Frank Brian, please visit the following sites:

For eBooks: Amazon.com

For paperbacks: CreateSpace.com/5103717

9788515R00175

Printed in Great Britain
by Amazon.co.uk, Ltd.,
Marston Gate.